'[An] amazing debut collection of short stories . . . [Colette Paul] writes short stories that are both more polished and far better observed than anyone has a right to d̶  ou *Choose to Love* is a guide, wl̶ ut next will at least be quirkily ̶d oddly true to life . . . This is a ̶, and – as her first books makes a ̶s well worth knowing' *Scotsm̶*

'Her book is thoroughly deserving of an audience. Her book consists of a dozen stories about couples and families, delicately exploring the relationships between them and often compelling the reader to ask questions that her characters won't ask of themselves or each other' Alistair Mabbott, *Glasgow Herald*

'Her skill is to make the mundane interesting and her characters likeable . . . her characters are cheerful, accepting and tolerant' *The Times*

'The stories are united by a wistfulness; a sense of disappointment acknowledged but not explored. And they're wonderful. Paul may be young but she understands a lot' Lottie Moggach, *Time Out*

'For someone so young, Paul's prose is stunningly perceptive. Her debut, *Whoever You Choose to Love*, is a collection of slick, quirky shorts which, despite the primarily domestic themes, have vast scope and cutting wit. Paul adds a modern, powerful spark to an oft-dismissed genre' *Esquire*

'An exquisitely carved short story collection . . . "outstanding" and "talented" are the claims on the back of the book. It's quite hard to argue' Brian Donaldson, *The List*

'Uncommonly affecting stories . . . a unique, pointed pathos' *i-D magazine*

'I couldn't put *Whoever You Choose to Love* down. It is brilliant. Funny, desperately sad, heartbreakingly recognisable, incredibly emotionally astute chronicles of human haplessness . . . Devastatingly truthful and written in delicate, tough, lovely lucid prose. Colette Paul really knows how to make a beautifully built short story' Liz Lochhead

Colette Paul was born in Glasgow in 1979. She has just graduated from the Creative Writing course of the University of Glasgow and is working towards a PhD.

Whoever You Choose to Love

COLETTE PAUL

PHOENIX

A PHOENIX PAPERBACK

First published in Great Britain in 2004
By Weidenfeld & Nicolson
A Phoenix House Book
This paperback edition published in 2005
by Phoenix,
an imprint of Orion Books Ltd,
Orion House, 5 Upper St Martin's Lane,
London WC2H 9EA

A CIP catalogue record for this book
is available from the British Library.

ISBN 0 75381 849 3

Typeset by Deltatype Ltd, Birkenhead, Merseyside

Printed in Great Britain by Clays Ltd, St Ives plc

www.orionbooks.co.uk

To my mum: best critic, best friend.

The author wishes to acknowledge the support of the
Scottish Arts Council for the purpose of writing this book.

Contents

We Are Broken Things

Eight o'clock on Saturday morning, I get a phone call from a woman in Elm Park Nursing Home asking me to come in and see them. She says it's about my father, Gavin Steele, and I tell her there must be some mistake, I've not seen him for years and years.

'No mistake,' she says. 'I've got really bad news for you, your father's passed away.' She says I should come in and see them as soon as I can.

I go back into the bedroom where Clive is awake now, sitting up.

'Any breakfast going?' he says, and I say I don't know, is he making any? I nudge him over so I can get back into bed. He says that he's a guest and he's starving. He'll fade away soon, and then I'll be sorry.

Clive is nine years older than me, although he doesn't look it, and he doesn't act it. A few months ago he joined the Socialist Workers Party, and now he spends all his time giving out leaflets, and going to meetings, and setting up campaigns. He says he's found his niche as a full-time rabble-rouser, and that work is just a lot of flapdoddle, exploitation, man is everywhere in chains etc. He says that in terms of wealth and status, in terms of society's definition, he knows that he's a loser, and that the sooner we recognize we're all losers, in one way or another, the better. We should celebrate and find strength in our loserdom.

I curl up next to him in bed and say I'll make something to eat soon, and he says that'll have to do, and lies down next to me. After a while I tell him about the phone call. How I'm now saddled with a dead father, a man I've only met once. It's a bit late, I say, to expect any filial duty. I don't think I'm going to go, I say.

Clive says of course I've got to go, he's still my dad.

'So?'

'Your dad's your dad,' he says. Then he ruffles my hair and says, 'You're a little tough nut.'

He's said this sort of thing before, and I play along because this version of me is acceptable to him in the way that tears and recriminations and declarations are not. He reserves that sort of thing for his ex-wife. He told me once that she was vulnerable. Fragile, he said. He actually used that word. *Fragile*.

'Like a piece of gossamer,' I'd said, and Clive said, 'Something like that.' He said, 'Don't talk like that about her, you don't know her. She's not like you.'

I make us boiled egg sandwiches and Clive fills me in on what's been happening with the Socialists. He tells me about a middle-aged woman they met on the street who was going home to make her kids' tea, but decided to go to the pub with them instead. She got drunk and started dancing with the cooked chicken she'd just bought tied round her back.

'What about her kids?' I say, and Clive shrugs and says who knows. 'What a character,' he says. 'She cracked me up.'

I make us another cup of coffee and put my arms round him, like a damsel in distress. I say he'll have to come with me to see my dad, I don't want to go alone. He laughs and wriggles away.

'No can do,' he says. He says he's got to head off, he's meeting Julie to discuss tactics for the People Against Closure of Govanhill Pool protest tonight.

'Stay a bit longer,' I say, 'you see Julie all the time,' and he says why shouldn't he, she's a friend.

'Do you find her attractive?' I say.

'Yeah, she's attractive. Nothing wrong with that, is there?' he says, and I say I suppose not. He says it's my pool too and I should come along tonight. Roddy and Bez are bringing dustbin lids to bang together, and some of them are dressing up in masks and stuff.

'There'll be loads of coppers,' he says, 'it'll be manic,' and I say that's a good word to use, *coppers*.

'Don't you call them pigs nowadays?' I say.

Clive says I don't take anything seriously. He smiles and says I need to find some beliefs, something I'd die for. He zips up his jacket and says he'll see me when he sees me. I shout back, 'Not if I see you first.' It's one of our jokes.

After he's gone I get back into bed and lie there for a while.

I go up to the receptionist and say, 'Gavin Steele's daughter.' It feels a strange way to define myself. There's something uncomfortably intimate about it. She smiles, then calls another nurse who comes round the desk and takes my arm. I don't like her chummy manner or the way I'm being manoeuvred down the corridor.

'You're Gavin's daughter?' she says, and I say yes, that's me.

I can't stop looking at her hair. It's long and blonde, permed up like a big swathe of candyfloss. There's something endearing about the misguided glamour of it, the rest of her so middle-aged and plain. We sit down. She tells me that Gavin passed away this morning, about five o'clock. When I don't say anything she says, 'It'll be a shock for you,' and I say, 'Yes.' She says they're all upset, Gavin was a favourite.

'He always had a joke or a quip for you,' she says. 'He joked me something terrible. We called him Ole Blue Eyes, like Sinatra, y'know.'

And then I realize she's starting to cry. I hate people crying in front of me. I hate the way their faces crumple and they look so defenceless, and that they don't care that you're there to witness it. I want to get them away from me.

'I'm sorry about this,' she says, wiping the corners of her eyes.

I tell her it's okay, she must have known Gavin a while, and she says again that she's sorry, you just get attached to them.

'He probably didn't feel anything,' I say, and she says no, it was a stroke. It was peaceful.

'There you go then,' I say.

She dries her eyes, and says I'll want to see him. When I say no, she says, 'Come on, it's no trouble. He's laid out for you.'

The room has faded flowery paper and smells of perfume, one of those room sprays. The bed's low with a chair beside it, a picture of a watercolour iris above. There's a table with a record player on it, and one record, *The Singing Detective*, and a Celtic football annual. It's a pretty mean bundle of possessions to go to heaven with. I avoid the bed and go to look out of the window. Two trees are beating in the wind, and the sky tin-grey. I watch some big white birds flying together until they're out of sight, and then I just look at the sky. After a while there's a creak from the corridor and I realize the nurse is waiting for me outside. I go over quickly and turn down the sheet. He looks peaceful. That surprises me. When Mum died her eyes were open, staring, and her lips twisted. I couldn't bear it, I couldn't go into the room again. The nurses will have cleaned Gavin up already. He's very pale, that waxy colour of potatoes, and he's bald. The time I met him he had thick black hair, so black it had streaks of blue in it. He told me it was his crowning glory, and that I was lucky to have good hair genes.

The nurse wants me to sit down. She asks if I want anything to eat, if I'll have a cup of tea. 'Have a rest,' she says. 'Take all the time you need,' and I tell her I'm fine, really I'm fine. I tell her I never knew Gavin, that I didn't have any sort of relationship with him. She says there's no need to explain, she doesn't judge.

'Some people judge,' she says, 'but not me.' She says it hits some people later on.

I was sixteen, summoned by a letter. Mum said it'd be his fancy woman's idea, it wasn't his writing. It was a cheek, she said, after all these years, but I should go if I wanted. She was more nervous than me when the day came. She was hanging up curtains, and then doing the ironing, then cleaning the bath, rigorous and deliberate as always. Yet I remember a certain stillness about her – not a calm, but the way her face registered no emotion, the way she carried herself so carefully, as if she was frightened to upset something dangerous inside her. Before I left, I put my arm round her and kissed her cheek. I caught her off guard and she jumped a little. It was a strange thing for me to do for we never touched each other. We were both embarrassed.

'What did you do that for?' she said, and I said I didn't know, I just felt like it. I said if I did it again, then she should worry. Then she should phone the nut house, and she said not to be daft and swiped me with a tea towel on her way past.

I had to get the thirty-eight bus, and get off at the Safeway on Giffnock Road. On the way there I didn't think at all about where I was going. I thought about what the boys on the bus might think of me. I was wearing a sheepskin coat from the Salvation Army, and a long patchwork skirt that I thought was slimming. I had blue eyeshadow on, and orange lipstick, the idea being that the colours would clash exotically, daringly. I wasn't sure if I looked glorious or monstrous, if boys would want to be sick on me, or cherish and love me for ever.

It took me over twenty minutes to find the house. It was set on the top of a high street, an eerily quiet street, with flies and bees buzzing over the gardens. The quietness struck me as sinister and deadening, and the houses grotesquely ugly in their uniform ostentatiousness. An architect's whim had allocated them each a different feature – wooden beams here, a latticed window there. I thought how Mum would love to live somewhere like this, in one of these houses, and it made me sad thinking of her in our flat, waiting for me.

It was a woman who answered the door. 'You must be Rachael,' she said. 'I'm Liz.'

She gave me a quick, erratic hug, and then grabbed my hand and rubbed it, saying to come in, come in.

I was expecting someone younger, but Liz looked about the same age as Mum. Her skin was a tangerine colour that creased and intensified at the corners of her eyes and neck. She was wearing a black lycra skirt with a low-cut lycra top to match, and her exposed skin looked sore and shiny, as if it'd dissolved.

'We've been so looking forward to meeting you,' she said, and smiled. She had a curiously vacant face that suddenly and extravagantly pulled itself into hieroglyphs of glee or surprise or shock, like a doll's. She ushered me down the hall, taking my arm in hers. I could smell her perfume, a heat of feminine effort, of skin powder and moisturizer, that was quite foreign to me.

'Your dad's in here,' she said, and opened the door with a kind of triumphant flourish. It was a few moments before he turned to look at me. He was reading a magazine.

'Well, what are you standing there for?' he said. 'Grab a pew.'

Liz went into the kitchen to make tea, and Gavin leaned back on the sofa. I perched beside him. The room was full of light. The carpet was a pale biscuity colour, and the walls a shade darker, with a yellow flower pattern. There was a real fire, flanked by white vases with thorny black twigs in them: it was studiously fashionable, like an expensive showroom display. The cream leather sofa creaked when I moved. Mum and I had gone into a furniture shop a few weeks before, for a look, and had seen one just like it. Mum had liked it. 'That's sumptuous,' she'd said, 'isn't it?' and I'd said no, I thought it was tacky. She'd said, 'Imagine having the money to buy something like that, it'd cost a king's ransom.'

Gavin asked me how I'd got there, and what I thought of the place. He asked if I'd seen the plaque outside the front door, and I said I hadn't.

'*Maison Lunatique*,' he said. Then he said, 'It means House of Lunacy. It's French.'

Liz came back into the room and said, 'Honestly, what an embarrassment he is. I wanted something like, I don't know, something nice, Bay View or something.'

She handed Gavin his whisky, and I saw her lightly touch his shoulder. There was something moving and pathetic about the touch, like he was an exotic flower that might wither if not treated with caution and gentleness.

'Thanks, wench,' he said, and she laughed and said, 'Oh, you.' She said he hadn't to give me a bad impression.

If Gavin was anything, he was robust. His face was red, like he'd taken a cheese grater to it, and he had a tremendous pair of jowls that merged into his neck. He looked like he was thinking about himself all the time, and quite satisfied with what he thought.

Liz told me that their daughter, Lisa, wanted to meet me, but that she was away on a school trip, and it didn't matter, there'd be other times. She said she was going shopping and would leave me and Gavin to get to know each other.

'Never mind what he says,' she said, 'he's been really excited about this. Running round the house like a headless chicken all morning, *Where's this, Where's that.*'

I knew that wasn't true, but that Liz wanted to believe it, as she wanted me to.

'Off to the shops with you, then,' he said, and gave her a lazy and imperious pat on the bum on her way past.

When the door had closed, he nodded towards it and said, 'She's an accountant part time and a glamour puss full time,' and he smiled an indulgent Sultan's smile.

'She's nice,' I said.

When he got up to pour another whisky I looked at my watch. I never had much to say at the best of times, and had no idea what I could ever find to say to *this* man. When he came back he said he'd have to have a good look at me, he hadn't had the chance yet. I said nothing. I was angry that he had the audacity, that he dared, to sit and inspect. He pronounced that I took mostly after my mum, but that I'd inherited his tendency to put on the bully beef.

'Don't blush,' he said, 'it's good to enjoy your food. No one wants a skinny bilinky. It's not done me any harm,' he said, patting his stomach.

He told me he had all the vices, eating too much, smoking too much, drinking too much. 'And the ladies,' he said. 'I suppose your mum's told you about that.'

'No, not really,' I said.

'Well, anything bad your mother's told you' – he lifted his hand and swept it over the air – 'it's all true.'

He put on a Rod Stewart CD and said we should have done this sooner, got to know each other. He told me about his job, some sort of managerial position in a company that sold inventions through a catalogue. He showed me a brochure and told me not to buy any of it, it was all crap. He asked me what I wanted to do, and I said I didn't know, which he approved of. No point jumping into something and being stuck with it till your brain shrivelled with boredom. Happiness was the only thing worth going for – you had to eke it out, spot the opportunity, jump right in there. It was like closing a business deal, and you had to be ruthless. People who were always whining and whingeing should get a bomb up their arse. He had no time for them.

Even if I had wanted to interrupt, I wouldn't have had the chance. He talked and talked and talked. It obviously pleased him to hear his voice, to hear his ideas take shape and gather round him; to discover, in the moment of articulation, another brilliant facet of himself.

'Now listen, thingummy,' he said. He took another drink and said, 'I'm terrible with names, don't be offended.'

'Rachael,' I said. 'My name's Rachael.'

'Now listen, Rachael. Live life to the full. Enjoy yourself. It's a decision, you've just got to make the decision. It's that easy,' he said, 'you've just got to decide,' and I said I'd try.

He said he could tell I was a thinker, and that I should work at not thinking too much. That was what was wrong with my mum, he said. She took too much out of things. He told me he wanted to go to Spain. There was a girl he knew in one of the towns there, Burgos, and she knew how to live. Dance all night, sleep all day, no inhibitions, no uptightness. No smack in the chops if you pinched her bum.

'And what a bum. Beautiful women out there,' he said, and made a curvy motion with his hands.

Liz came back at five and served dinner, a big Sunday roast thing with four courses. She wanted Gavin to stop drinking, but he wouldn't. She argued with him in a cutesy, coquettish way, and looked at me, rolling her eyes and saying, 'What can I do with him? See what I've got to put up with.' She asked me if I had a boyfriend and I said no.

'You will,' she said sympathetically. 'Give it time.'

She said she knew someone who knew Carol Smillie at school and none of the boys ever asked her out, but look at her now. 'She's an envy now.'

Gavin reached over the table and took some carrots. He told Liz to stop being daft, I was fine as I was, and Liz said she knew that, she was just saying look at Carol Smillie now. She said, 'Don't take too many carrots, sweetheart, you don't like them.'

'I love carrots,' he said, and she said, 'But they don't love you.'

Before I left, when Gavin and I were in the sitting room together, he said he wanted to give me something.

'You're a reader,' he said. 'Am I right? You look like a reader,' he said, and I said yes, I liked some books.

'Over there,' he said and gestured to a bookcase along the back wall. 'Pick anything you want.'

'No thanks.'

He said to go on. He didn't know what was there, they were mostly Liz's, but there'd be something to catch my fancy.

'No, I'd rather not,' I said.

'What's wrong with you? Go on.'

It seemed to take me hours to reach the bookcase with Gavin watching me. The spines blurred together, and I grabbed the nearest one, shoved it in my bag, and thanked him.

Gavin drove me to the bus stop. He would take me right home, but they were meeting a couple for drinks. The bus stop was empty, and it was past nine o'clock. I walked round and round the shelter. I took the book out of my bag and shoved it in a bin. I felt hollow, whittled away, and was upset to see my reflection, sullen and fat, unchanged and staring back at me.

He never contacted me again, except for the Christmas cards. When Mum died, I phoned his old number and Liz answered. She told me he'd gone off to Spain a few years back, and she didn't have his address. She said she was sorry about the way he had treated me, and I said not to be sorry, I didn't care.

'You know, Rachael,' she said, 'he broke my heart like an eggshell,' and her voice began to waver. If I found out his address, could I let her know? She said she knew it was wrong, but she still loved the bastard. I said it wasn't wrong, but she should try to move on. For her and Lisa's sake, she should try to move on.

'I'm sorry about your mum,' she said. 'I really am.' She said, 'You'll be okay, you're a survivor. I said that to Gavin, "That girl's a survivor," you know, back when you visited us.'

Gavin left when I was three. I don't remember anything about him. Once, when we were doing family pictures at school, something came to me. A man holding my hand as we walked past the launderette on Pollokshaws Road. He was so tall, and the sun so strong, that his shadow carved a way in front of us. That was all. Mum said that he was big, built like an ox, but that I was still in a pram when he absconded. She never talked about him much and the only time his absence was recognized was at Christmas, when he sent a card. Every year, scrawled on the inside, *Xmas Salutations To You All*, and Mum pierced the top with a pen and threaded ribbon through the hole. She hung it up on the Christmas tree. She'd stare at it for ages and then say, 'He's still an atheist, then,' and I'd say, 'What's an atheist?'

'Someone who doesn't write Christmas,' she'd say, and then we wouldn't mention it again. Mum was from the minimalist school of conversation. She found yappers tiresome, and said she often glazed over if forced to listen to one.

One time, when I was about fourteen, the card that came was one of those group photographs, Gavin standing in front of a Christmas tree with Liz and Lisa sitting on either side of him –

although I didn't know, then, who they were. Mum sat down at the table to study it.

'Would you look at that,' she said, and gestured me over. 'I wonder how long this one'll last.'

Everyone in the picture looked too hot. The girl beside Gavin looked about ten, with curly butter-yellow hair. Mine was dark and poker-straight like Mum's.

'She looks like a dish rag beside Gavin,' she said, pointing to Liz. 'I don't see it lasting,' she said. 'I don't rate it.'

And then she tore the card up and threw it away. I got the pieces out of the bin and tried to fit them together. It was no good. I tried to remember what he looked like: his hair bushy and triangular at the front, temples glistening like they'd been oiled. He had a nose that was maybe like mine, flat and circular at the front. And he looked happy. The type of person who would roar with laughter, and roar with anger too.

I told Mum she shouldn't have torn it up, the card was addressed to both of us, and she said sorry, she hadn't thought.

'Why didn't you tell me he was fat?' I said.

'Does it matter?'

'No.'

'Well then. Don't bother me just now,' she said, 'I'm not in the mood.'

Later she came into my room with a shoebox full of old cards, all folded back into their envelopes. She said I might as well have them. I looked through them, urgently at first, then bored. I couldn't understand why she had kept them. They all said the same, *Salutations All*. I found something reassuring about that. Like a Roman Emperor booming through to us, arms spread open, encompassing: *Salutations All*.

She never kept the cards after that one, and it was only when I was older that this struck me as strange. She must have been sad, but I wouldn't have dared to ask her, and she never said. I didn't understand her way of coping with life, didn't understand her motives, and all my attempts to get closer to her, to urge her into revelation, were frustrated. I used to ask her what she was like at my age, what games she played at school, did she have a best friend?

'I had a cat named Snowy,' she'd say. 'I loved Snowy.'

'What about school?' I'd say. 'Were you ever bullied?' and she'd say no, she didn't think so. She just played skipping, and went to church and knitted, like the rest of the girls. And I'd say, 'What else?'

'I just told you.'

A year or so after I'd finished my degree I came back home to look after Mum. She was really ill by that time, lying on the couch most days. One morning, while I was brushing her hair, she said we needed to talk about what would happen when she died. She said it couldn't be avoided and it was best I knew where everything was, what kind of arrangements were to be made. She didn't want to be cremated because the idea of burning scared her, although she supposed it wouldn't matter to her by then. We were silent for a while, and then she said I'd make a good nurse. She said she didn't usually like people too close for comfort, but that she didn't mind me. Then, out of nowhere, she told me that when she and Gavin were first married, she used to dream that he'd have an accident. She would have to look after him, and he wouldn't be able to go anywhere without her.

'That's terrible,' I said.

'I know,' Mum said. 'Love does terrible things to you.'

I said it would have been a good thing if someone had hospitalized him, he was such a bastard. Mum said he wasn't all bad, she'd got me out of the whole thing. She said she'd always loved me, and that she was worried she hadn't been a good mum. I said of course she had been. She was.

'I'm not very open,' she said, 'to emotional things. I never hugged you very much, or anything like that.'

'Mum,' I said, 'you're not a hugger. Neither am I.'

'Give me a hug now,' she said, and I did.

I get home about four. The street lamps are on, blurred in mist, and all the rooms in my flat are cold and dark. I make a cup of tea and sit in the living room with it. I think of the whole night ahead, alone, and think of things I can do: clean the bathroom, wash out the kitchen cupboards, water the plants. But I don't do any of this. I phone Clive a couple of times, and get his answerphone. Then I phone an old friend from university, whose flatmate tells me she's out. I phone Clive again. I do some washing, I put on a Bob Dylan record. I lie down on my bed, and smell him on the pillow.

Mum had waited up for me the night I met Gavin. From the street, I looked up at our flat and saw her bedroom light on. I dreaded having to see her. I went straight to my room although I knew she'd been waiting for me. I didn't know what her expectations were, or how to fulfil them. The burden weighed me down. Anyway, she could come to me for once. It was five minutes before she knocked.

'What do you want?'

The hall light revealed her thin and drawn in the doorway, and I felt ashamed when I saw her, exposed, and needing me more than I needed her. She said she'd just made some tea, and bought us both a cake, if I wanted to have a chat.

'It's a cream slice,' she said. 'From that fancy bakery.'

I said I didn't want anything. All the things she took tiny pleasure from – a new shampoo, the Fair Lady figurine collectables, a cream slice – seemed to me pathetic and small, not enough.

'Can I come in, then?'

'If you want.'

She sat down slowly on my bed. 'So how is he?' she said, and I said he was fine.

'Did he look well, though?' she said, and I told her that if being four stone overweight and having a big red face was looking well, then he looked well.

'He always had a flush to him,' she said. 'What did you talk about?'

13

There was something urgent and coaxing in her voice, her head bent forward, that I didn't like to see in her.

'He talked a lot, I didn't. He talked about his job, selling stuff from catalogues, home improvement kind of stuff. He said he was big in the company.'

She smiled and said that would suit him down to a tee, he could talk the hind legs off a donkey, and I said he certainly could.

'He was drunk, too,' I said. 'He was so drunk he cut his hand with the carving knife.'

I thought that would shock her, but instead she said, 'Oh, his hand.'

'*Oh, his hand.*' I impersonated her as cruelly as I could. Then I said, 'For goodness' sake, get a life.' I looked straight at her, and didn't say any more. The bones in her neck jutted out, the bones in her arm as she gripped my bedpost. It made me sad, and that annoyed me. Mum should be stronger. I said I didn't see how they'd ever had anything in common, that I thought he was disgusting. I yawned and said I was going to sleep.

She knocked an hour later saying she was sorry to disturb me again. 'I was just wondering,' she said, 'did he mention me at all?'

'No,' I said. 'Nothing. You'd have thought he'd at least ask.'

'Right then,' she said. 'I'll leave you now.'

I couldn't sleep afterwards. I got up and went into her room. I said that I just said it to spite her. I said that he did ask after her, he said she was the love of his life, but they just couldn't make it.

It all came out wrong, sounded exaggerated, sarcastic even. She turned her head against me in the darkness and said, 'It's okay. Go back to bed.'

I stayed where I was and didn't know what to do. 'That wife's got nothing on you,' I said at last. 'She's mutton dressed as lamb.'

'It's fine,' she said quietly, 'go back to bed.'

At eight o'clock I begin to hear noises from the protesters at the Govanhill Pool. Tribal sorts of drums and people cheering. I stand by the window and listen to it, watching the lights flicker on and off in the church across the road. *Christ Died For Our Sins*. I think of Mum buried in Rutherglen Cemetery, lying there in the dirt, and Gavin dead too, waiting to be disposed of somewhere else, never to meet again. Maybe Mum was holding out for a celestial reunion in heaven, I don't know. I'd like to talk to her again. I'd like to talk to her about anything. I'd like to say just, 'Remember that ... remember this?' And I think even saying those words out loud, so personal and lovely, would make me feel better.

I phone Clive again, and still don't get an answer. I text him to stop saving the world and give me a call. Then I text him again, writing, 'We are broken things.'

I watch some telly with the phone beside me.

I was just back from university, and on my bed, crying over a boy. Mum had come into my room, even though I said she couldn't. She said what was I doing that for? and I said I didn't want to talk to her. She gave me a hanky and told me to stop leaking. She said it wasn't good to get too dependent on people, look what it did to her.

'Look at me,' she said.

'I'm not you,' I said. 'I'm not like you.'

She said a tip she found good was that every time you think of that person, say red onion to yourself. And if you keep saying it, red onion red onion red onion, you start thinking about red onions instead of that person. You start thinking about what they look like and taste like, and what dishes you could make with red onions.

'Try that,' she said, and went out, closing the door behind her.

I go down to the pool. There are police lined up against the building and only a scrappy group of protesters left. It's raining, and I don't have a jacket on, and I can't see Clive. I walk around, hoping to talk to someone, but most people are making their way

15

home. I stay for about twenty minutes, until I'm standing there alone. A policeman tells me to go home, there's nothing to see.

I go straight to bed and sleep. I have terrible dreams. Hundreds of different eyes clicking open and shut at me. When I wake, I'm terrified. I have to sit still and remind myself who I am, who I am, and that everything's fine, everything'll be okay.

I'm Happy, You're Happy,
We're All Happy

Oliver did this thing with his eyes. You know how you sometimes see pictures of saints or nuns with blurry, soft-focused pupils looking heavenward, well it was like that. When he did this I always wondered what he was thinking. He had another pose too. Head down, eyes shut. He had the darkest, gravest eyelids I'd ever seen. The first time we went out for a drink together he told me he had one blue eye and one green eye.

'Does it bother you?' I said. I was amazed I'd never noticed.

'If it's fine by David Bowie,' he said, 'it's fine by me.' He was playing with a butt in the ashtray. After a few minutes he said, 'You've got nice eyes too.'

I said I'd always thought so, but no one had ever confirmed it. It was a joke, but he didn't realize, or if he did, he ignored it.

'You've been hanging around with the wrong people then,' he said.

I first saw Oliver in Burger King. He was new, so had been put on broiler duty. He was feeding the machine with frozen discs of meat and then sandwiching them between rolls as the burgers came flopping out the other side, bubbling fat and blood. It was the worst job. The grill dripped strings of yellow grease, which sizzled off the boiling metal; the whole machine trembled and steamed. Your face went blotchy after a few minutes beside it. Sweat glistened in your hairline, in the creases of your nose and chin. But Oliver was looking very cool about it. He had a nonchalant way of doing things. He gave the impression that he could saunter away at any moment, like he was only exerting the minimum of effort and that's why he stayed.

None of the staff liked him. They thought he was arrogant, and too big for his boots. They had a field day when he slid on a French fry and had to be taken home. It was his own fault, they said. Those daft boots. He just had to be different, and look where it got him.

His cowboy boots were regulation black, so the manager couldn't tell him to change. They had silver stars on the side and heels that tip-tapped on the floor. I wasn't there when he fell, and can't imagine it. Can't imagine him having to be helped up, supported between two people, dependent.

Don't get me wrong. It wasn't that Oliver was handsome or anything. In fact, he had two of the pointiest incisor teeth I've ever seen. He wore his hair ridiculously greased up, matador style. It was the way his face changed all the time. I watched for its alterations. I couldn't decide if he was ugly or handsome, so kept studying him to see.

I was too shy to sit in the staff room and would sit by myself in the dining area. One afternoon he came over and sat down. He didn't look at me and sat eating his Whopper. Then he said, 'What are you reading?'

I held up the front cover, embarrassed, and angry with myself for being embarrassed.

'Egon Scheile,' he said, leaning back on his chair. 'It's pretty obvious what his paintings are about.'

'Yes,' I said, although I didn't know what he was talking about. It was just a book I'd picked up in a jumble sale and had liked the look of.

He said he was a painter himself. He was trying to finish his portfolio for September. He said that every year he went off to a remote Scottish island where he drew and painted by the sea. He said how strange the people were up there. How none of them had driving licences but flew around in their cars like bats out of hell. They knocked down squirrels and grouse and retrieved them from the road, cooked them for dinner. He described red-nosed men slumped paralytic outside the weekly ceilidhs.

'Lot of queer hawks there,' he said. 'I was in good company.'

Surprising myself, I said, 'It can get lonely with normal people,' and Oliver said, 'Darn Tooting.' He said he liked my style.

We never really went out. I was unsure of where the boundaries lay, what could be said and what could be assumed. It was ages before I plucked up the courage to invite him to my flat. For weeks I'd imagined making a meal, thinking about what I'd cook, how I'd throw it all together in front of him, drinking red wine from a mug. There would be candles, and chiffon draped over my lamp. The squalor would be beautiful. We'd look at my books piled carelessly along the walls. Imagining this night was one of my favourite pastimes. As it was, he came up one night after work. There was a thunderstorm on the way over, black clouds sank forebodingly over the streets, one bruised strip of light above us. We were soaked by the time we got home. My flatmates were in the kitchen so we went into my room. The window was open and there was cold air and rain pummelling into the room.

'It's freezing in here,' Oliver said. 'Can you not shut that thing?'

I told him it was jammed but I'd put the fire on. It wouldn't ignite, and the room stank of gas and burnt matches. Oliver sat on the bed with his arms wrapped around himself. He prided himself on his thinness, how his hands could meet round his back. I could tell he was annoyed at the cold, and that annoyed me, so we both said nothing for a while.

'Why don't you come and lie down,' he said at last. 'You've nowhere to sit over there.'

'Yeah, okay. It's quite uncomfy down here.'

I undid my trainers and put them to the side, eased myself on top of the bed. I tried not to look at his boots dripping mud and dirty water onto my sheets. We lay side by side, and after a while I said, 'I saw that girl you used to go with today.'

'Yeah?' He turned to face me. 'What was she doing?'

'Shopping, I suppose. It was in the St Enoch Centre.'

He wanted to know who she was with, so I described the girl.

'That'll be Anna,' he said. 'I can't stand her. She was never a good friend to Catherine.' Then he said, 'How did Catherine's skin look?'

'A bit sore. Is it acne she's got?'

'Catherine's got terrible problems with her skin.'

He said this to himself, just loud enough for me to hear. He had his head down and looked so sorrowful I wanted to reach out and touch him.

'Do you think you'll ever get over it?' I said, casually.

'Yeah,' he said, 'but I don't know about Catherine.'

He looked straight at me and said he wasn't looking for a relationship just yet, though.

'I want a bit of fun first,' he said.

'Yeah,' I said, 'you don't want to be tied down or anything.'

He began to stroke my ribs and I listened to the rain pound outside, dropping onto the floorboards under my window.

Sometimes, before work, we walked through the park together, or down Allison Street into town, or we picked a street we didn't know and followed it to see where it ended. Oliver liked the early morning. The streets were always long and bright with unbroken shadows. It was December, just before Christmas, and the trees had been stripped bare, the pavements glistening with ice.

'Clears the cobwebs,' said Oliver when I complained about the cold. 'Feel that air,' he said, and he abandoned his face to the wind. His hair came loose and flapped off his forehead until he smoothed it back. He looked out of place everywhere. His funny clothes, his lean ravenous face. Too fragile for all his swaggering, and that's why it was attractive, because it was a stance, it was striven for.

'If people are going to think you're odd,' he said, 'you might as well go the whole hog.'

I felt closest to him on these walks. Oliver talked about his dreams, which fascinated him. He had one where T.S. Eliot phoned him and introduced himself as Tom, and Oliver asked him how it was going, and they had a chat. He recited Oliver's favourite poem, the one that goes,

O dark, dark, dark. They all go into the dark, the vacant interstellar spaces,
the vacant, into the vacant.

Oliver said the poem was the funniest thing he'd ever heard, he said it pretty much summed up his life view. I said I preferred Stevie Smith's *Smile, smile, and get some work to do*, and Oliver said that was a good one too.

We played games where we imagined what people around the world were doing at that very moment. Olga in Moscow, famous for her sweetmeats, was decorating a cake that depicted the fall of the Berlin Wall; Pierre, a fraud inspector in Nice, an apologetic man who perspired a lot, had just found his wife in bed with his brother. Millions of births and marriages and divorces and people getting it on. People discovering they had cancers, breaking up, making up, getting drunk, sleeping, eating. A couple in this street, Mary and Brian, arguing about a basil plant Brian chucked out because it was cluttering the place.

I asked Oliver his favourite colour, favourite song, favourite anxiety.

And all the time I could feel my blood move around my body, feel the electricity in my brain, I could feel and hear and see everything. All the life in everything was pulsating and alive and growing and enriching. The sky was more blue, the grass more green, noises were truer, human beings were nobler and greater and more beautiful than they would ever know. But it was only because Oliver was there with me. The mornings settled in, people made coffee, stared, thought about the day ahead. We wandered aimlessly. It was a conspiracy of sorts: nowhere to go, no one to go to.

'We're both solitary creatures,' he said one morning. 'People who are meant to be alone.'

I was horrified and said that I wasn't, or I hoped I wasn't. 'Speak for yourself,' I said.

'I mean, *I* don't need anybody,' he went on. 'Sometimes knowing that makes me feel guilty, and sometimes I think, well why should I? What good does it do you? Sometimes I think, more fools them. I wouldn't give up my freedom for all the tea in China.'

Oliver was always talking about his freedom like it was some physical attribute you either had or you hadn't, something you could lose or misguidedly relinquish. He said he'd sacrificed it for Catherine, but never again.

'You wouldn't give up your freedom for all the farms in Cuba,' I said.

'Nope, not for two birds in one hand.'

'Not for a cloud with a silver lining,' I said, 'or the crock of gold at the end of the rainbow. Red sky at night, shepherd's delight,' I said. 'Too many cooks spoil the broth.'

'I think you're taking the piss now,' said Oliver.

I told him to listen to Janis Joplin: *Freedom's just another word for nothing left to lose*. I said what if chasing freedom's another form of being unfree, of being trapped?

'You could have a point there,' he said.

I had made friends with a girl I worked with in Burger King. Before I met Oliver, Clara and I had started going to pubs together, sometimes to nightclubs. She was the only person I'd got to know in Glasgow. I didn't make friends easily, not even acquaintances. Oliver said it was because I didn't smile much. Like Russian prime ministers in the old days, he said. They didn't feel the need to grin all the time. He said it was what had attracted him to me.

Clara laughed like there was no tomorrow. Her teeth were too big for her mouth and made her lips stick out, obscuring everything else about her face. Her skin was ragged and coarse like it'd been raked over, but she didn't cover it up with make-up.

'This is me,' she said, 'the whole woeful package.'

Everything Clara did was accompanied by noise. She talked as fast as she could get the words out, she roared with laughter, she exclaimed loudly, she dropped things, she was always tripping over paving stones or jamming her fingers in doors. It wasn't ostentatious, intentional noise but a kind of edgy, desperate nerviness that she was always trying to beat back. We spoke about our parents and our trials and tribulations at school, and how we hated Burger King, and our money problems. We talked about boys we liked, and how we didn't know why we liked them, and wondered when any of them were going to like us back. Clara was in love with a boy who worked in Safeway and she'd make us walk down there and buy something so she could see him. We always went to the cashier three tills down from him because Clara was scared to talk to him. She'd wave over and he'd smile bewilderedly back.

'He thinks I'm a nutcase,' she'd say, 'but I can't help myself. See that lazy eye he's got, I just love him for that. He looks so sad, I'd just like to cuddle him up to my bosom.'

'Clara, you are a nutcase,' I'd say.

I saw Clara less and less when I started going out with Oliver. I liked to be available in case he wanted to see me. One Saturday, when Oliver hadn't phoned, I called her and we arranged to meet in a café. She had dyed her hair a funny red colour and was wearing a brown-checked bonnet of her dad's to hide it. She was upset about a boy who'd said he'd phone her, but hadn't.

'I even slept with him,' she said, and I said she should know by now that that didn't guarantee anything, far from it.

'What is that supposed to mean?' she said.

'None of these boys ever phone you,' I said. 'I'm scared you're getting a reputation. And I hate seeing you doing this to yourself when you're better than the whole lot of them.'

At first Clara didn't say anything. She sat still with her

23

shoulders drooping, and the silly hat on, and I said, 'Clara, I'm not trying to hurt you,' which I wasn't. I just thought I was being honest, like friends should be.

Then she said, 'You're jealous.'

Her voice was getting louder and louder and the conversations around us were dropping off.

'You're jealous,' she repeated, 'because boys want to sleep with me' – she put her hand to her chest like a damaged bird – 'and not you. Because you're stuck with that nincompoop who couldn't give a bat's fart whether you live or die.'

'Listen,' I said, 'forget what I said. Maybe you're right just having fun. Clara,' I said, 'just calm down.'

She stood up and said, 'If you want some honesty, let's start with you. Everyone but you knows you're making a fool of yourself. You love him all right, but does he love you?'

'I don't know,' I said.

'Well that's fine,' she said, 'but you should sort yourself out.' She said, 'I don't want to be your friend any more. I don't think I need friends like you.'

I went straight round to Oliver's flat, uninvited. I'd never done that before.

Oliver was a minimalist. He said he liked knowing that he could move on any time he wanted. In his room there was a single mattress on the floor, a chair beside a desk and a chest of drawers, and that was it. I sat on the edge of the mattress. I told him Clara and I had fallen out and that I didn't think it was my fault, but maybe it was. Oliver didn't say anything. I said she was my only friend and I'd blown it, and she hated me now. Pitied me, which was even worse. I didn't tell him what she'd said.

Oliver sat down beside me. 'She's not worth a hoot,' he said. 'There's other fish in the sea. When one door closes another one opens. If you don't laugh you'll cry,' and he got me to wipe my face and stop crying.

He put his hand, just quickly, on top of mine, and said, 'Just you and me against the world, eh?'

His hand on mine. I couldn't think any more. I wanted to kiss every freckle on his skinny arms and say, thank you. Thank you, thank you.

We started going to Queen's Park, where Oliver sketched and took photos of swans for his portfolio. He never finished anything because he kept tearing the sketches up in moments in frustration.

'That tree was all wrong,' he'd say, or, 'I've spoiled that cloud that was meant to pull the picture together.' He was ruthless.

He only painted swans. He started a new one just before he left. Two of them in the park, the taller one nestling the other in the crook of its curving white neck, protectively. They were as white and still as unmarked snow. He had ten in all. Swans in various settings. Untouched and untouchable white necks, like they'd just been cracked open from alabaster moulds. Some flamingo-pink, floating in murky rivers, one on a window ledge looking down on urban decay. I laughed at him choosing something as genteel, as decorous, as swans, and Oliver, annoyed, said they were beautiful with a huge capacity for viciousness. He said he wanted to be a swan. They didn't get concerned about anything, just did their thing. He said maybe he'd live somewhere far away, with a whole gaggle of them doing their thing and he'd do his.

'What would that be?' I said, and he said he didn't know.

'You're more like a walrus than a swan,' I said. 'Walruses are sort of grand because they're so foolish-looking, but don't know it. They're never going to be what they think they are. Also, I imagine them to have independent spirits.'

Oliver laughed. 'If you had to be any animal,' he said, 'you'd be a baby elephant.'

'Thanks very much.'

'They're gentle and very loyal,' he said, 'like you.'

'Loyalty's not much to have going for you,' I said.

At the start of May both our leases ran out and Oliver said it would make sense to get somewhere together.

'It'd be cheaper,' he said. 'It'd be okay.'

We found a room, a converted roof space, at the top of an old house on Joy Street. The name appealed to me, although there was nothing joyous about the place. Rambling old houses in various stages of dilapidation lined the street like rotten teeth that refused to budge. Next door to us was a derelict old folks' home, half the windows smashed, a pram and discoloured mattress in the back yard. At night kids would congregate there, smoking and drinking cider. One morning I woke and they'd graffitied the side of the building next to our window: ARMS ARE FOR EMBRACING, and below, WE DON'T WANT YOUR BLOODY WAR, and then, obscurely, poignantly, JOHN F LOVES ME.

The landlady, Mrs Reilly, lived downstairs with her husband Stan. Oliver and I shared a bathroom on the second floor with the other lodger, a man called Mike who never spoke to any of us. Sometimes he put his hand up in a gesture of hello, and sometimes he didn't. When he had a shower he always left a note on our door: *Please don't enter the bathroom for the next fifteen minutes as I will be showering and naked. Thanks.* He wore tight leather trousers and a biker jacket, and he played Morrissey and The Fall and opera music all night long. Oliver said he seemed the type of person who might have scrapbooks full of movie stars' pictures. We invited him up to our room a few times, but he never came, and soon we stopped asking him.

Downstairs, where Mrs Reilly lived, was like a war zone. The mess was awesome – a door propped against the wall in the kitchen, welts of brown sludge running up the bath and down the walls of the bathroom. There was fusty wet washing lying in the crook of a dirty velvet settee, old cat litter piled in the hall, a splintered church pew, sea shells, stacks and stacks of dusty *Daily Records*, plastic carrier bags. The house smelt of old vegetables and animals. I counted ten cats at one point, although they were always coming and going, some being reclaimed, others disappearing, new strays arriving. They darted about, tense-backed and wary, scratching at doors and walls and each other. Mrs Reilly left bowls of food and water all round the house for them. She told me she was a sucker for strays.

When we first moved in we made up fanciful and unreasonable stories about Mrs Reilly. We imagined her the rich pampered daughter of a textile mogul, fallen on hard times. Mrs Reilly had inherited his crumpling empire, had been left all alone in the world with only her dreams and her charm at her disposal. She had been jilted once, and terribly, had married Stan on the rebound, a man who knew how to be restrained with his words, who loved her grandness, her excess. We could talk like this for hours.

'One day, there'll be no more stories,' I said to Oliver one night. I put on a mock-sad voice. 'And what then? What shall we do then?'

'There'll always be stories,' said Oliver.

Oliver didn't like Mrs Reilly, and he hated the cats. He said they made his allergy bad, and gave him the creeps. He had quit his job at Burger King and was staying at home, trying to paint. I was finding it hard living with him. Some days he hardly spoke. He said speaking was a waste of time. He said Kierkegaard gave up talking when he realized how meaningless it was. Oliver was going one better. He gave up movement, never mind talking. He said it was a political decision.

'If you don't move,' he said, 'you can't affect anything.'

I asked Mrs Reilly if she'd mind trying to keep the cats away from our room. 'I would if I could,' she said, 'but it's their house too.'

She kept leaving bowls of cat food on our landing, and Oliver would grimly empty them out of our window. After a few weeks the cats stopped coming near our door, and I suspected Oliver had been kicking them. I thought he was capable of that.

Mrs Reilly, I soon realized, told lies. Not big, important lies, not even lies that made her look better, but the kind that made you wonder why anyone would waste their time telling them. Once she told me that she'd been followed home from the shops by a man wearing a trilby, although I'd heard her in the kitchen all day. Another time, she said a baby chicken had fallen into her plate when she cracked her egg. I told Oliver to listen to her for sheer entertainment value, her whole theatre of emphatic gestures and flourishes when she told her stories. Her eyes would dash around, searching for a wider audience, even though there was just me and Oliver in the room, and Oliver would turn his back on her, or pointedly read a book. She wore wigs – blonde, brunette or red – and depending on the colour she would say that she'd always thought, really, that she should have been a blonde. She'd put her hands to her face coquettishly and ask me what I thought of it, and I'd say it suited her.

'Monroe eat your heart out,' she'd say, 'there's a new girl in town.'

One afternoon she confided in me that she wore the wigs because her hair was falling out, and it distressed her. Bald patches the size of plums all over her head. I knew this wasn't true because I'd seen her coming out of the bathroom one day, and her hair was wet and streaming down her back. Black, and no bald patches. What was funny was that the wigs weren't even glamorous, but old-fashioned, brittle and imperturbable. They were shaped into bouffant styles that wartime mothers might have worn, perched at a jaunty angle, like tea cosies, on top of her head. Also, I only ever saw her in slippers, pale pink, spiky-heeled ones, with tufts of marabou at the front. Drag queen slippers, Oliver said.

We'd hear her stomp around restlessly downstairs after Stan had gone to work. And then, the creaking of the stairs.

'Here comes the Madam,' Oliver would say. 'I'm out of here.'

And I'd sit and listen to them pass each other, in silence, on the stairs.

'Hello, dear, I'm just up to see how you are.'

'I'm fine, Mrs Reilly, and yourself?'

This was her cue to tell me exactly, and with great detail, how she was. 'Well you know how it is,' she'd start off, touching the corners of her mouth with her great sausage fingers. 'They think it's down to the surgeon's knife now. A h-y-s-t-e-r-e-c-t-o-m-y. Will I just sit down for a minute ...'

I came to dread hearing her knock because it meant Oliver would go out, sometimes not coming back for hours, or else he'd be in a bad mood all day. We'd stop what we were doing and sit very still, or I'd peek my head out of the door, doing as much as I could to bar her. But nothing put her off. She sat heavily on our bed, her cigarettes and ashtray balanced on one knee each. She told me true-life stories she'd read in a magazine (a woman whose sister bit off her ear; a woman whose husband was actually a woman; a woman addicted to Spam) and how she liked a cracker with pâté at eleven o'clock every day, wasn't that funny? and that the couple at number twenty were breeding rabbits just so they could watch them copulate.

'Maybe they're pets,' I said, enjoying the ridiculousness of it.

'When you get to my age, love,' Mrs Reilly said, 'you get to know a pet lover from a pervert. No,' she said, 'you just keep to the other side of the road from them.'

Oliver got into terrible moods. He would cry for days and days, sitting on a chair and letting the tears fall until his eyes were raw. It distressed me more than him, I think. I begged him to tell me what was wrong.

'Nothing,' he would say. He said he didn't want my help, he wanted me to go away.

'But I've nowhere to go,' I said.

'Just go away and I'll be fine.'

I put my hand on his back and he shook it off and told me not to fucking mother him.

'If you don't want me to mother you, then don't act like a fucking baby.'

Sometimes I'd storm out, but once outside our bedroom, I realized that I really did have nowhere to go, no one to go to. Clara was still ignoring me at work. So I'd go round the block and then back in. One time he apologized. He said he should treat me better, but that he was a depressed person, he was never going to be happy.

'Don't look at me like that,' he said. 'Don't look at me so pitifully. It's chronic,' he said, 'not terminal.'

A day later, or even a few hours later, Oliver would be in a good mood. His face would be animated and jumpy, as if someone was pulling strings connected to pulse points behind his bones. Then we could talk all day. We spoke about our futures, but always solitary futures that didn't involve each other. That made me sad. Oliver wanted to own a travelling library that he'd drive to a new place every day. He would live in the library, and everything had to be wipe-clean, and able to fold away entirely. That was important. I said I'd grow massive, prize-winning marrows, and Oliver said forget the travelling library, he'd be a famous artist. There'd be spoons given out on national holidays with his face on them.

'No,' I said, 'I think you'll just become a common pedestrian little human being. You'll get fat, and have a mouthful of bad teeth and be unashamed.'

'Common!' Oliver said. 'I'd rather die.'

He ran over and pulled me into his arms, into a Hollywood romance pose.

'We'll have no more of this talk,' he said. 'Okay?' he said, and I said I couldn't speak, I was swooning.

'Quite right,' he said. 'Carry on.'

We stayed in our room almost all the time. Twice a week I worked double shifts in Burger King, starting at seven and ending at midnight. On those mornings, I would wake up early, about half five, and lie in bed, looking out of the window at the sky clay-white, violet-streaked. I'd stare for ages at the ARMS ARE FOR EMBRACING graffiti, the only bit of the wall I could see from our bed. Such a strange feeling came over me, those days, a feeling that was oppressive and overwhelming, sorrowful and buoyant at the same time. I still can't describe it.

The room was dusty. There were gargantuan roses crawling up

the wallpaper, a tiny sink, a hob, a chair with the telly on it. The brown singed carpet stopped a few inches short of the wall. Everything we owned was on the floor. We fought about the mess, but then we fought about everything. I remember one argument about Melvyn Bragg's hair. It escalated so suddenly, violently. I remember Oliver saying that was it.

'Fuck this,' he said.

He ran over to the telly and shoved it as hard as he could off the chair. The telly was especially important to me because I watched it all day when Oliver wasn't speaking to me. In a kind of blind rage, I grabbed his special Elvis record and tried to bend it. He ripped my Bob Dylan poster. I chucked his boots out of the window. Oliver said I was pathetic, always wanting people to like me, and it made him ill.

'You're the one with no friends,' I said, and Oliver said he didn't see people queuing up to talk to me.

'Only that mad hatter downstairs,' he said. 'And you're so grateful. Slobbering like Pavlov's dog when she says she'll show you how to make soup. You're just another one of her strays,' he said.

I called him selfish, a big baby. I said he always felt sorry for himself and it was pathetic. He couldn't stand to be denied anything. He couldn't take responsibility for himself, for anything he did. Oliver said at least he was honest.

'Well you,' he said, 'you thinking you're such a nice person when you don't even like people that much. You just want them to like you. That's fraudulent. You've got a bullying streak. That's why we're in this shit-hole,' he said. 'Because you were going on and on, you thought it'd be a good idea. I had no choice.'

And so it went till we were both crying, both out of breath, spent, looking round at the mess. And we said truce. I went out to the back to find his boots, and when I came back Oliver was huddled on the bed.

'I don't know about you,' he said. 'You don't anchor me in reality.'

'What d'you mean?' I said. 'What does that mean?'

He said Catherine had been like a reality check for him, like the canary you take down the mine with you. She let him know when he was in trouble, when he was getting too crazy.

'But you're crazy too,' he said.

I said everyone was crazy in their own way, he shouldn't let it bother him. We went for a walk, and I put my arm through his. We walked for hours, no moonshine, the streets getting darker.

At times, yearning for Oliver made me almost weak. I wanted to touch him, but was afraid to, like a light switch I knew would give me a shock. I named parts of his body as mine. A hairless strip of skin on the back of his shin, one stray black hair coming out of his sharp shoulderblade.

'You're going to make me loathesome when you go,' I said.

Rain began to batter against the window. I thought he'd gone to sleep, and was watching him, a little bit asleep myself. Suddenly he asked me if I loved him.

'Yes,' I said. 'Do you love me?'

'I think so. How much do you love me?'

'Till the ocean is folded and hung up to dry.'

'That's okay then,' he said, and shut his eyes. Soon he was asleep, and I, still a bit asleep myself, continued to watch him.

About two months before Christmas, almost a year since we'd first known each other, Oliver didn't come home. It wasn't until the next night that he turned up.

'Before you start,' he said, 'I've got something to tell you.'

He was going to Grenoble to work in one of the ski resorts. They were desperate for staff. Good wages, and a beautiful place to work. They were going to pay his flights and everything. He could be away before Christmas. He hated Christmas.

'Where did you hear about this?'

'From Catherine,' he said.

He'd met her the other day on his way back from the library.

They'd gone for a drink, and started talking about things. He didn't tell me, but I knew he must have spent the night with her.

'And is she going? Are you going together?'

He said there was a bunch of them, all friends from school. He was leaving five weeks on Monday.

'Hey, don't cry,' he said.

'I'm not crying.'

He said he was sorry. He thought I knew the deal.

'The no strings attached idea?' I said, and Oliver said yeah.

'I like you a lot,' he said. 'I might even love you, whatever that means. But you always knew I wasn't over Catherine. I never lied to you.'

I said I was actually happy he was going, and he was happy to be going. 'We're all happy,' I said. 'Happy happy joy joy. So why don't you just beat it.'

Oliver said he wasn't going to leave it like that. He said, 'Come on, it's late,' and lay down on the bed.

'Come and tell me one of your stories,' he said.

The next day I told him to get out. I said not to phone me, not to come round. 'This is our goodbye,' I said, and he said, Okay.

He said, 'Take care.'

The next night I went downstairs. Mrs Reilly was in the kitchen reading *Woman's Own*.

'What's wrong, pet?'

'Just left me,' I said. 'I don't know what to do.'

Mrs Reilly came over and smothered me in her arms. She said she'd known something was going on.

'Just left me,' I said. 'I don't know what to do.'

Mrs Reilly said it wasn't the end of the world, even if it felt like it. She said it happens all the time, all the time, and other people manage, and I said no. No, she didn't understand.

'Sit down,' she said, 'I'll make some tea.'

She said I was too good for him, she could see that. There was no life in him.

'We understood each other,' I said, and Mrs Reilly said I'd find someone who understood me better. 'Don't speak to him,' she said, 'don't talk to him. If you've got a cancer, cut it out.'

She sat with me for hours, until I was worn out and could hardly lift myself from the chair.

'Scoot,' she said and nudged me towards the stairs. 'Get some sleep.' She shouted up that I'd to remember he was a fool.

'You don't get many of you in a lucky bag,' she shouted.

For a week I lay in bed, absorbed in my own grief. Everything in the room reminded me of him. I re-ran conversations we'd had, wondering if anything I'd said, or hadn't said, would have made a difference. I didn't eat, was sick, didn't sleep. I got sacked and didn't care.

Gradually, things started to get a bit better. I got a new job in Freezways. I worked with a fifty-five-year-old woman who sat in the back all day, smoking menthol cigarettes and thinking up things for me to do. I worked in a trance, puzzled that my body had not shut down, puzzled that I was still able to function, put on make-up, talk, eat, catch buses. I washed the freezer lids with water and vinegar, and mopped and buffed the floor till it gleamed. I listened to the steady buzz of the freezers all day long, and was sullen and disagreeable to customers. Oliver would've approved. I managed to get through days, and then weeks.

The Monday when Oliver's plane was leaving, I couldn't sleep. I got up and dressed and took the earliest bus I could get down to the airport. It was three days before Christmas and the place was decked in tinsel. There was a massive tree covered with glass baubles, and hundreds of people moving all at the same time, in different directions. I suddenly felt dizzy, as if I were about to faint. I made my way forward to read the departure board. A plane for Grenoble had already left but there were more throughout the afternoon. I sat in one of the visitor lounges. If they passed, I'd see them but they probably wouldn't see me. That's what I wanted. By mid-morning the crowds had thinned out and then it was busy again about lunchtime. Someone came and asked me if I needed any assistance and I said, 'No, thank you.' 'Check the board,' she said, 'that tells you about any delays.'

By five, all the lights were blazing and the plate glass reflected me back to myself. I thought, I'd better go home, but didn't have the energy to move. I thought, I'm not going to cry, but then I was.

Here, This Tragedy

Edith gets up early, before Susie is awake. She starts running a bath and walks through to the sitting room. It's seven o'clock, bright outside. She pulls back the curtains and stands, caught in a net of light, enjoying its feel on her skin. The street's empty, but for a man walking his dog. He stops at the Pawn and Cheque shop, and bends down to squint through the window shutters. He stays like that for a few minutes, transfixed, the dog patiently at his side. As he walks away he bangs the grille with his fist. It makes a harsh, metallic sound, then everything's quiet again. Edith watches him till he turns the corner into Allison Street. Overnight some of the closes across the road have been graffitied, and the bus-shelter's been trashed as well. It happens every few weeks, or sometimes every few days. It doesn't depress her this morning, as it sometimes does. The days when she thinks, *You can keep it*, and won't go out, stalks around the flat thinking up activities to fill the day, feels a sharp sudden anguish when she can think of no more to do, when she runs out of activities before lunch.

Today feels different, imbued with possibilities. She thinks of Toby and their date tonight. In the kitchen she eats an orange, looking at the flowers she painted on the edge of the cupboard. Then she looks at her geranium plant, precarious atop a pile of old cookbooks that she never uses. With the stillness of the morning, and her expectations of the day ahead, the things around her seem foreign and new, beautiful in themselves, and she wants to reach out and touch them. Toby's house is much tidier than hers. It isn't hysterically masculine – no brooding greys and charcoals, no black wood, no barren walls – but it isn't feminine either. She thinks it suits his kind of unemphatic maleness, his long hands lightly haired that could fix a watch or move a wardrobe, the bones pushing and flexing under his skin. He has a collection of squat beatific Buddhas, a menagerie of Buddhas, sitting on top of a cast-iron fireplace, and a bust of Plato at the end of a bookshelf, and plants everywhere in pots spray-painted silver. Edith tells him it's easy to tell he doesn't have kids.

'That off-white carpet,' she says, 'that would've gone a long time ago.'

She notices that nothing ever moves from its given position in his house, that everything external to him must be ordered or else becomes an impediment. She tells him about her flat. She tells him about the mismatched carpets left by the previous owners, the old TV, the dripping kitchen tap. She exaggerates because Toby seems to like to think she's eccentric and chaotic, not giving a damn. She says he should loosen up a bit, should embrace a bit of discordance and cacophony in his home, and Toby says he needs cacophony like he needs a hole in the head.

'Plants wouldn't be allowed to wither here,' she says. 'You'd whip them up and sort them out before they had time,' and Toby, smiling, says, 'Indeed I would.' He uses words like that a lot – *indeed, certainly so, perfectly serious* – gentlemanly, assertive words whose very assertiveness is undercut by the edge in his voice, as if he thinks their claim to authority absurd.

In the bath she puts a deep conditioner on her hair and shaves her legs, taking excessive care. She rubs her skin with rose-scented soap and an exfoliating cloth, enjoying the rituals purely for themselves, with no illusions about being transformed once they're over. She thinks she knows about her face now, that she's plain but not without her good points. She looks young for her age – people say they can't believe she's got a nineteen-year-old daughter – her skin still fine and tight across the bones; her nose, chin and forehead prominent so that she looks over-exaggerated, startled. Last week Toby'd said she had an interesting face. They were having dinner in Boozy Rouge on St Vincent Street. Clair was watching Susie. Edith had licked her soup spoon and Toby laughed and said, 'You're not supposed to do that.'

'Why not,' she said, 'I'm enjoying it. It's a life-affirming act,' she said, and Toby said restaurant etiquette was against it. She joked about it, asking the dear-gentleman-sir if he could teach her the ways of a lady, but afterwards she felt self-conscious. They sat in silence for a while.

'What are you looking at?' he said, and she said, 'Nothing.'

He said he always wondered what she was thinking, that sometimes she seemed a million miles away. She said she didn't think she was thinking anything, or not anything interesting.

'You've got a metaphysical face,' he said. 'Like you're reflecting on things not visible to the human eye.'

'That's nice,' she said. 'I'll use that for my personal ad: skinny brunette in her forties, teenage daughter with learning disabilities, metaphysical face. I'm a real catch,' she said, and he said he thought so.

'Well, what do you think about?' she said. 'You don't give anything away.'

He looked around, wiping his mouth, and then said, 'Death.' They both laughed, surprised at the baldness of the statement. He went on, saying it wasn't dying he was scared of, it was death itself. It was being obliterated for good, wiped out, annihilated, forgotten.

'The way I see it,' he said, 'there's no after-life, no reincarnation, no airy-fairy heaven-hell malarkey. You're just put in the earth, you dissolve and then worms eat you.'

Edith said she'd heard that was what religion was for, she'd heard it was good for that sort of fear.

'Tried it,' he said.

He said he'd tried them all, he'd even read the *Koran* once. Didn't think he could afford to reject any of them. He couldn't believe, and Edith said neither could she. She said after Susie was born she didn't trust any more that the world was benign, or that whoever had made it was good. She told him she remembered coming out of the doctor's. Susie was only about two, and she'd taken her because she wasn't speaking yet, she wasn't walking. She was thinking that she was being over-anxious, that the doctor was just going to pat her on the head and tell her not to worry.

'That's what was at the back of my mind,' she said.

But the doctor had seemed concerned too. He'd done all these tests on Susie, eye-tracking tests and all that sort of thing. And then, when he'd finished, he said he thought she might have learning disabilities, just like that.

'And I remember he was looking at his nails at the time,' said Edith, 'and I was looking at him looking at his nails. He was doing it absent-mindedly. I always remember that. And he said Susie'd have to get more tests, that he couldn't tell how bad she was going to be, and I didn't say anything the whole time. I was in shock because Susie looked normal, just normal and lovely like any baby. So, he set this date for us to go back, and he told me about people who could help, about the options I had, full-time care – this was nineteen years ago and there was Lennox Castle, places like that, big institutions you could shunt people off to . . .'

She stopped, conscious of talking for too long. 'I'm boring you?' she said, and he said no. She said she wasn't used to talking about herself for so long.

'*Open lips sink ships*,' she said. 'That's what my mother used to say if she thought we were talking too much. Anyway,' she said, 'when I got outside there was this sky everywhere and people going about their business. And it was like – what d'you call that painter, the one with Icarus falling from the sky?'

'Breughel?' said Toby, and Edith said, 'Yeah, that one.'

She said, 'It felt like here this tragedy had just crashed over me and no one in the whole world could see, no one was bothering their arse, no one cared. So I just walked on, pushing the pram, and there was no one I could call and tell. I just walked on as normal, like you do.'

She told Toby it was then, in the space of going to the doctor's and coming home, that her whole life changed. She didn't believe in anything after that.

When she stopped speaking, she was embarrassed. Toby was looking at her very intently, he was looking at her with his whole face. She laughed to disperse his attention.

'That must have been when I got my metaphysical face,' she said.

He said it must have been terrible for her, did she ever think about giving Susie up? and Edith said no, of course not. If anything, she loved her more after that. Toby looked away and said it put what he was saying into perspective. He said, 'Let's not talk about this any more, let's only have pleasantness,' and Edith said okay.

'Pleasantness and niceness from now on,' she said.

The soap disperses in the greyish water and she stares as her knees rise out the water. She's listening for Susie waking up in the other room.

Over breakfast she tells Susie they're going out with Toby today.

'We're going on the bus,' she says, 'and then to look at pictures, what d'you think of that? Does that take your fancy?'

She rubs Susie's nose with hers, and Susie laughs, her chin dropped onto her neck and her lips pushed back so her teeth show. Edith says Toby's heard all about her and her antics and he's dying to meet her. Susie grabs her arm and brings it up to her head so Edith can stroke her hair. You're a terrible girl, she says, and Susie smiles again. 'Hair,' she says, and Edith says yes, her lovely hair. She says they'll do it up nice today.

In the bedroom Susie picks what she's going to wear, and Edith sits her down to put on her make-up. She holds her face up, her lips squeezed together, and Edith gets a sudden urge to kiss her, the way her face is caught in the light, pale and round as the moon, exposed towards her and waiting to laugh. She kisses her two scrunched-up eyes, and then puts on the lipstick, some pink eyeshadow.

'Look,' she says, pointing to Susie's reflection in the mirror.

'Who's that beauty there?' she says, and Susie moves her face close to the glass and laughs.

Edith can never tell what's going on in Susie's head. When she laughs there seems nothing behind the laughter but happiness and enjoyment, and when she frowns there seems nothing behind the frown but displeasure, and Edith can't predict what'll make her laugh and what'll make her frown. All her moods write themselves over her face, in the way she furls her forehead or holds her lips, a universe that's whole and impenetrable, its origins incomprehensible to her. The other night when Edith had checked up on her, she'd found Susie in her nightdress, standing by the window, looking out. Edith'd stood with her, pointed out the stars, asked her if that was what she was looking at. Her eyebrows were creased in a sort of parody of quizzicalness. She'd told Susie to make a wish, and then she'd tucked her in again, and Susie had shut her eyes. Later, in the sitting room alone, Edith had remembered a poem they were taught at school. An Irish poet whose name she couldn't recall. It was something about the man looking up at the sky, the wind blowing, and him asking himself, What is a star, what is a star.

Toby rings the buzzer at two. Edith opens the door of the flat, listening to his footsteps on the stairs getting nearer. She feels herself tense, ready to spring open like a jack-in-a-box.

'Here we are then,' she says. 'Come in,' she says, and Toby says he might just do that. He gives her a chaste kiss on the cheek, a gesture that makes Edith uncomfortable. It's the formality, the bloodlessness, of the kiss. It makes her feel curiously condescended to, like he's bestowing a favour on her. She takes him through to the sitting room where Susie's walking up and down the middle of the floor. Toby shuffles from foot to foot and then comes over, his hand out. Susie looks at him for a few minutes and then grabs his hand, squeezes it. Edith laughs and says that's a good sign, she must like him.

'We tidied the flat for you,' she says. 'Didn't want you coming into Dante's Inferno, did we Susie?'

'It's fine,' says Toby. 'You've given it an unfair press.'

She goes into the bedroom to get her and Susie's jackets, and a few minutes later Toby follows her in. He says he was embarrassed, Susie kept looking at him and he didn't know what to say to her.

'Just talk normally to her, like you would with any human being. Don't just ignore her,' she says, and Toby says he's sorry, he isn't used to this kind of situation.

They get on the forty-four bus, her and Susie on the front two seats and Toby behind them. Susie presses her face to the window and Edith tells her to watch out for dogs. She turns to speak to Toby. He's been in Venice for two days, taking over some Whistler sketches for an exhibition. They'd been forgotten when the rest of the paintings were taken over. They had to be carried in a special briefcase, with him escorting them all round Venice, a kind of James Bond mission without the weaponry and women and shady adversaries.

'I had to examine the space they were going to be hung on, check the light was right, make sure the room temperature was perfect. It was quite a big responsibility, they're insured for thousands and thousands of pounds, and . . .'

'Woof woof,' says Susie, and Edith turns back and says, 'Yes, that's right. You like that dog, Susie? What were you saying again, Toby?' she says, but he says it doesn't matter, it wasn't important, and he looks out of the window.

A woman carrying a baby round her stomach gets on at the next stop and sits beside Toby. Edith watches Susie look at her.

'Baby,' says Susie, cradling her hands together. 'Baby.'

Edith smiles at the woman, who smiles back. 'A lovely baby, Susie,' she says, and before she can stop her, Susie's hand shoots out towards it. The woman jolts back in her seat, and Susie's hand just brushes the baby's leg.

'Susie!' says Edith. 'You've not to do that,' and she turns to the woman, apologizing. She says that Susie loves babies, she wasn't trying to hurt him, she just gets excitable.

'That's not what it looked like to me,' says the woman. 'She could've had his leg off.'

An old man a few seats away shouts, 'Come and sit over here, love,' and the woman gets up and goes over.

'You're better away from people like that,' he says, loudly, so the whole bus can hear. Edith looks over at him and shouts back, just as loudly, that they're better away from people like him. 'You old bastard,' she shouts.

Susie wrinkles up her forehead and grabs Edith round the neck, dragging her forward and pretending to cry.

'What's the matter with you, Miss Worried?' says Edith. She strokes Susie's hair and talks about the pictures they're going to see, how they'll have a cake afterwards. She looks at Toby who's gone a roast beef colour, staring straight ahead, his jaw clicking. He whispers to her that there was no need to make a scene, the woman was just concerned for her baby, and Edith says there was every need to make a scene.

'Making a scene doesn't help change attitudes,' he says, 'and neither does bad language.'

'You can bugger off too,' she says.

They get off the stop before The Hunterian Gallery.

'Let's not spoil our day,' she says, and Toby says fine by him. He says he detests scenes, and she smiles and says he talks as if it had been a gladiatorial fight or something.

'I don't think we should go to the museum,' he says. 'It's kind of quiet there, there's a lecture theatre downstairs and they don't like people being noisy.'

'We're not noisy people, are we Susie?' says Edith. She can almost smell Toby's discomfort; she thinks he may even be sweating. He says that all the same, he doesn't really want to go to his place of work on his day off, and she says fine, they can go to a café instead.

They go to the West End café, sit in a booth that closes them all up together. While she's in the middle of telling Toby about a book she's reading, he interrupts her, screwing up his face and saying, 'You'd better watch her, she's just stuffed that whole thing in her mouth.'

'What?'

'That whole slice of pizza.'

That moment, with perfect comedic timing, Susie starts to choke. Edith rubs her back till bits of goo start flying out of her mouth. Just as the coughing subsides, a big bit of chewed pizza lands on the arm of Toby's coat, and he sits looking at it for a few minutes. Then he starts to laugh, and so does Edith. Susie looks at them, frowning, and pushes away her plate with the pizza still on it. She reaches over to Toby's plate, grabs his yum-yum, and starts eating it.

'My bloody yum-yum,' he says laughing, making Edith laugh more. 'I was really looking forward to that yum-yum. I could weep,' he says.

He waits outside while she takes Susie up to Clair's. Clair runs to the window to try and get a good look at him, and Edith, laughing, says, 'Don't, he might see.'

'So what, I'll give him a wave. Ask him if he's got any pals for me,' she says. She makes Edith promise to tell her everything, all the juicy details, and Edith says there'll be no shenanigans of that sort.

'He doesn't know you're taking Susie overnight,' she says. 'I'm just going to see how it goes.'

She says all that sweating hands romance stuff is for teenagers, and Clair says, 'Away you go.' She says she can't remember the last time a man wanted to get his mitts on her, and that she should enjoy it before he starts farting in front of her and expecting his dinner.

'I don't think Toby ever farts,' Edith says. 'Or if he does, he deals with his emissions very discreetly, very privately.'

'They all fart, hen,' says Clair.

'You'd laugh if you met him, Clair, he's something else,' she says.

'But do you like him?' Clair says, and she says yes, she doesn't really know why. Clair says she doesn't need to know why. She says Edith should bring him up sometime, and Edith says maybe she will one day.

She gives her Susie's overnight bag, the Topaziate and the Eplin. She tells Susie where she's going and gives her a hug. She worries a bit, standing by the door, saying bye to Susie again. She's sitting down and not looking at Edith.

'You know Susie doesn't go in for bye-byes,' Clair says. 'Off you get and have some fun.'

She waits till Edith's out the door and shouts down, 'And remember, if you can't be good be careful.'

Downstairs, she finds Toby with his hands in his coat, looking around him. He says he thinks he can safely say, not a very salubrious area, and Edith says they can't all live in the rarefied air of Newlands. She says he's got no idea how ordinary people live. She goes to say more but stops herself.

They walk to the main road and he hails a cab to take them to his house. On the way Edith tells him she always worries about leaving Susie even though Clair's great with her. She says it's stupid but she always gets upset that Susie doesn't say bye to her, that she doesn't seem to care they're being parted.

'It's just a habit,' says Toby, and Edith says, 'Yes,' and then, 'No, not really.' She says that if she were to burst into flames right beside Susie, Susie would just stand and watch. She'd be upset, she'd be anxious, but she wouldn't do anything. She wouldn't be irrevocably sad, she'd get over it and still be happy. Toby says she shouldn't talk like that, she shouldn't worry. Edith thinks of Susie curling up on Clair's sofa, her body shifting and settling till she's comfy, her hands on her lap like the queen. She smiles thinking of it, Susie positioning herself just so, as if she were settling down to survey her empire.

Toby says he's tired. He's quiet, and goes into the kitchen, leaving Edith sitting by herself. They eat a Thai curry he's made, eating it from trays on their laps, watching *The Truman Show*. He sits on the armchair, and she alone on the sofa. Through the bay windows the sky's gone striped, yellow and green, and Edith says if she were an artist, that's what she'd paint. Toby tells her that once, when he was at university, he'd gone out with a girl who cried all the time. Whenever she saw a beautiful sky, or saw wintry trees with snow on them, she would cry. She could cry at anything. And he tried to see what she saw, but never could. He'd just see sky or trees or whatever, and she'd say, *But really look, just concentrate on looking*, but he still couldn't see anything but sky or trees: for him, they never transformed themselves.

Edith says that's funny because he works with art all the time, and you'd think he'd have a better eye than most people, you'd think that visual stuff would move him more than ordinary people. Toby says he's just good at the technical stuff, art movements, brush-strokes, art history. He glances at her, and then glances back at the television. The film's near the end, the bit when Truman's trying to escape out of the TV world, and the producer's sending down tidal waves and thunderbolts to stop him getting across the water.

'Go Truman, go,' says Edith, feeling silly when Toby doesn't respond. 'Is something wrong?' she says.

'Nothing's wrong, really,' he says, and his voice sounds disembodied, unconnected to him, as if he's been dubbed. He tells her that the girl at university wanted to marry him and he thought that was what he wanted too, but it turned out it wasn't really. It transpired he couldn't do it. He couldn't deal with the thought of emotional commitment, that even getting physically close to her, even though he loved her, was terrible for him. He'd sweat with worry beforehand, it was terrible for him.

Edith doesn't know what to say. She asks what happened to the girl and Toby says she got married the next year. He wasn't upset, he was relieved.

'She had a lucky escape,' he says.

He says, 'The thing I'm trying to say, the thing I'm trying to explain to you, is that I've had opportunities before. I could have got married and had children and all that, but I didn't. I look and I see that I've laid waste to my life, haven't done anything, haven't produced anything, but it couldn't have been any other way. I've made my life to suit who I am. That's what I'm trying to say. I'm trying to say that I'm just like this, I don't want change. I don't want disturbance.'

'Is this to do with Susie?' Edith says, looking at her plate. 'Is this about what happened today?'

He says today just made him realize. It made him realize that he was being unfair to her, that he was going along with some illusion that they could be a normal couple, that they could be a happy family out in the world.

'Can I stay the night?' she says.

She doesn't know where her words come from. She doesn't know if it's the kisses in the film, the comfort of a body for the night. She doesn't know if it's because he's been crying the whole time he's been talking, tears coming down his cheeks, and suddenly, for the first time, she feels her heart move towards him, something huge with no words to explain it.

'Can I stay the night?' she says, hardly believing what she's said.

Toby says he doesn't think it's a good idea, and she says, 'No, it isn't. I'm sorry,' she says.

'I'll be going then?' she says, and he nods.

Supernovas

After tea Dad says, 'Fancy a trip to the observatory?'

Mum sighs and starts collecting up the dishes. 'Can't you stay at home just one night?' she says. 'Is that too much to ask?'

Dad tells her it's shooting star season, and besides I've never been before. 'It'll be educational for Cat,' he says. Outside a car horn beeps and Dad says, 'That'll be Maya. You'd better go put on something warm, Cat.'

I run upstairs and get my Aran jumper. When I come down, Mum's sitting at the table herself, smoking a cigarette. 'Your dad's in the car already,' she says.

'Why don't you come?'

'I've not been invited,' she says, staring ahead. She finishes off her wine in one gulp, and then she turns and smiles at me. 'Anyway,' she says, 'I've got things to do.'

The car horn beeps again and she says, 'You'd better go. Have a good time.'

I ask Maya to drive faster and faster until we're going at eighty-seven miles an hour, and then I ask her to slow down because I begin to feel sick. Dad says so does he. He says Maya's a maniac, and she laughs like that's a compliment.

'It's a good job you weren't going that fast when you mowed me over,' Dad says.

Every time Dad and Maya are together they make jokes about how they first met. Dad was cycling to Granny's house when Maya cut in front of him, and sent him flying off his bike. She ran

48

over to see if he was okay, and Dad sat up and said he thought she owed him a drink. So they went for a drink.

'It was cheaper than an insurance claim,' Maya says.

I like Maya. I like her hair, which spans uncontrollably all round her face, and her heavy jewellery that she lets me try on. I like how she makes nasty jokes about everyone except me, whom she treats as her conspirator. Some of Dad's friends I've not liked. I didn't like Carol, who clutched his arm and laughed at everything he said; I didn't like Rosetta, with her puffy, moon face and her broken English. When Rosetta came over for dinner she only said about five words the whole night, and when she left Mum said she was drugged up to her eyeballs, and that Dad had never to bring her over again. Dad said that Rosetta didn't know anyone here, and that she just didn't have a very expressive face, but I never saw her again after that.

The observatory is very cold, dome-shaped like the sky. We climb a lot of twisting stairs to reach it, and it's empty when we get to the top. Our voices echo. Maya and Dad stand beside me while I look through the telescope. Maya did a degree in astronomy so she knows more than Dad, who's just an enthusiast. She points the telescope so I can see the constellations – Orion, the Bears, Cassiopeia. I can't join the stars together. No matter how hard I look they just remain scatterings of stars, tiny, bright specks of dirt. Maya says it doesn't matter, you should spend time just looking at the sky, not trying to find things. But I get bored.

'Tell me about shooting stars again,' I say, and Maya describes the sky pitch-black, and the stars hot-silver, their tails flashing as they hurtle to earth. People trace the fall of shooting stars, they collect them when they land on earth as lumps of stone.

'Can they fall on people?' I ask, and Maya says they can but it's not very likely. I imagine black stones scattered all over the snowy North Pole, and Eskimos picking them up, scratching their heads and wondering where they've come from. The stories about stars are better than actually looking at them. There are supernovas – dying stars, dazzling, exploding stars – and black holes, which frighten me.

'No one can see black holes,' says Dad. He's not spoken for a while, and has been waiting for his chance. 'You only know they're there because of what happens around them. And if you fell into one, you'd disappear. You'd be swallowed into it for ever and ever.'

A black hole in a black sky is difficult to imagine. It's like trying to imagine your hand disappearing through a mirror. Dad smiles and his teeth flash.

'It blows your mind,' he says.

I move to the side and Dad and Maya take turns looking through the telescope.

'Are there any stars,' I ask, 'that no one's ever seen before?'

'Yeah, lots,' says Maya. 'We can only see very little.'

Dad says that if he discovers a star he's going to call it Mycat, a cross between our two names.

'What about the wife?' Maya says. She always calls Mum that and laughs, even when Mum's there.

'Ann can get the second one I discover,' says Dad. 'There's a whole galaxy out there, there's no need to ration them.'

I've to stay in the observatory while he and Maya go down to the car to get the beer they've brought. They're away for ages and ages, and I begin to get cold, and frightened by the dark. I wish I was back at home with Mum, but then they come back and it's okay again. We sit against the wall, and Dad and Maya drink beer from bottles. I ask Dad for a taste, and he says, 'Why not,' and hands me his bottle. The beer tastes horrible and I can't drink it the way Maya does, the bottle tipped back as if it's water. She has one bare foot, with red toenails, dangling over her knee. She raises her knee and kisses it, and the bells on the bottom of her dress tinkle.

'Mmm,' says Dad. 'That looks good.'

Her dress falls away from her neck and her bones shine mild blue, as if her skin could be pierced like tissue paper.

'This is the life,' she says.

*

On the way home Dad says that whatever happens in the observatory is secret. There's a code among astronomers.

'So don't tell Mum,' he says.

I nod, although I've no idea what I'd tell her anyway. Dad puts on his Iris Dement tape and sings along.

Easy's getting harder every day.

Maya rolls her eyes and says she hates these whiney songs. Outside there's endless dark, with stars spangled everywhere. It's warm in the car, and I shut my eyes. Dad reaches over and smooths his hand down my hair.

'It's nights like these,' he says, 'that make up for how appalling life is the rest of the time.'

When he wakes me up, we're parked outside our house with the car lights off. Dad looks at his watch and says, 'Ten minutes to midnight, it's nearly my birthday.'

'Forty tomorrow,' says Maya. 'It's all downhill from here.'

'I'm in my prime,' says Dad, patting his stomach. 'You're coming to my birthday bash tomorrow?' he says.

'Oh God, do I have to?'

'Yes, you have to. Ann's already bought in the cheesy balls.'

'Oh well, in that case,' she says. 'There's nothing I'd love more than to spend my Saturday night with your wife, stuffing cheesy balls into my gob.'

'That's the spirit,' says Dad.

Mum and I get up early to make Dad a special birthday fry-up. I'm in charge of the toast and tea, and Mum does the rest. I get out the tray, and arrange the food nicely on the plate.

'You take it through,' I say, but Mum says she's got to iron our outfits for tonight.

'I won't have time after work,' she says.

Dad's asleep when I go in. I put down the tray and jump on top of him, singing 'Happy Birthday'. He wakes up and I give him the card I've made. It has stars all over it and in each star is something that happened in 1952 when he was born. He studies it carefully before he says anything.

'Well, you've outdone yourself here, Cat,' he says in a serious voice.

He shouts through to Mum that they've got a genius on their hands. He looks at the card again and laughs, and Mum comes through and tells him how it's all my own work.

'Come and sit down,' I say. 'We need to watch Dad open his presents.'

'I don't have time,' she says, standing by the door with her hands round her waist.

'Two presents,' Dad says, 'from my two favourite girls.'

He's in the middle of the bed, rising out of the sheets like a big hairy Neptune. Three weeks ago, when he was coming out of a phone box, a man head-butted him and knocked out his front tooth. He tells people about it in a way that makes them laugh, although it's scary, not funny. He says to people he can't afford a new tooth, but Mum says that's not true.

She gets him a book about meditation and I get him a bracelet I made myself out of dried melon seeds. He puts it on right away. He says he's very fond of both melon and reading, and Mum says he's very lucky then.

At ten o'clock Mum goes to work, leaving instructions of what we've to do around the house.

'You don't have to make all this fuss,' says Dad. 'Maya doesn't care what the house looks like.'

'I care,' says Mum. 'I know rich people like Maya don't have to bother about tidying their houses, but I care.'

When Mum leaves, Dad and I watch the *Pepsi Chart Show*, and then we play draughts. Dad talks about a children's book he and Maya are writing about meteorites. It's a market, he says, that's not been exploited before.

'We could do a whole series,' he says. 'Meteorites, the star signs, the moon.'

He says I could read them over and give them feedback from a child's perspective; Mum could give up her job and do the illustrations.

'I've got a really good feeling about it all,' he says.

Mum did a degree in art, and there are pictures she's painted all around the house. There's one of a woman with her back turned, looking at the sea, and another one of the sea being tossed and turned and a man walking his dog along the shore. Mum says that the sea was her speciality at art school, and that there wasn't much market for seascapes when she left. She started working at Hazel Dean, and she's been there ever since. Dad says she should chuck it and devote herself to painting, and Mum says she'd love to, but who'd pay the bills? And anyway, she says, she's not very good any more.

'You are, Mum, you're brilliant,' I say, but Mum just smiles and shakes her head.

Sometimes Mum gets annoyed about Dad not having a job. She brings home recruitment papers, but Dad never reads them. He says he's an ideas man, and that creative people like him shouldn't be tied down to mundane things. He's a thinker, not a doer.

'Try writing that on your passport,' Mum says.

Some of Dad's ideas are good, but they don't last very long. For a while, though, it's all we talk about: keeping goats for cheese, selling his knobbly rustic-look chairs to a big retail store, jewellery made out of forks. We all get caught up in it. Mum helps him draw up schemes, plans of action. She talks about approaching banks.

'Maybe this'll be it,' she says, and Dad says he's sure it is, he's never been surer.

'Truth be told,' he says, 'that goat thing was doomed from the start. We got carried away. But this candle idea . . .'

For a few weeks the miracle of it makes Mum and Dad light-hearted, and we all laugh and talk. The world is full of free-floating marvels, and you can just reach out and claim one. It happens so effortlessly. But something always goes wrong, and then I hear them arguing. Last month it was about the jewellery made out of forks. Dad had bought two hundred forks and three pairs of craft pliers, and then decided, a few days later, that it wasn't such a good idea after all. The forks wouldn't bend properly, or else they snapped in the middle. The four pendants he made were ugly and too heavy, and none of the shops he took them to would buy them.

'What're we meant to do with the two hundred forks, then?' Mum shouted.

'We'll use them,' said Dad. 'We can give them to people for presents.'

'Give them to people for presents! Happy Christmas, here's ten forks and see you enjoy yourself! I don't believe this. We can't even pay the electricity bill.'

She put her head down on the table and started to cry, and I hate it when Mum cries. She cries like there's no tomorrow, and her whole body shakes up and down.

'I don't know why I ever married you,' she said. 'I must have been off my head.'

'Come on, Ann, it'll be okay,' said Dad, hugging her.

Mum was only eighteen when they met at Gran's house. Dad was twenty-seven and already divorced. He came round the door to sell life insurance and left with a wife. That's how he tells it, anyway. I've heard it told four or five different times, always in slightly different ways.

'So I got the wife but, alas, no sale,' he'll end, and look forlornly at his hands. Other times he says: 'I dusted her down and plucked her off the shelf.'

Mum told me one day that she already had a boyfriend when she met Dad. We were sitting at the kitchen table, waiting for Dad to come home.

'What happened?' I said.

'I done the dirty on him,' Mum said, in a serious voice that made it sound like she was talking about some natural disaster. She told me I should never treat anyone the way she did, and I promised I wouldn't. Ross worked in the Co-op with her, and was so small and skinny he looked like he was starving. His head was shaved because he was going bald, and that made him seem serious, which he wasn't.

'What did you say to him when you broke up?' I asked.

'I told him I'd met your dad.'

'Did he cry?'

Mum said he didn't cry, he didn't really say anything, although she knew he was hurt. And then, two weeks later, Dad proposed.

'And that was me,' she said.

Dad came home, and Mum told him she was telling me about Ross, and how Dad proposed two weeks later.

'Do you remember,' she said, 'you were standing at my mum's front door? It was raining and I wanted you to come inside, but you wouldn't. You said you needed to know. It was all part of the theatre, of course. You were soaking and you looked so urgent, and I thought, "Well he must really mean it. You wouldn't do that if you didn't mean it." And you said, I'll always remember, "Eat the peach," and I said, "What the hell does that mean?" and you said, "It means go for it." Go for it.'

'Did I?' said Dad. 'Well, it must have done the job.'

'You got me good and proper,' said Mum.

'Now who's this you've brought to grace our company?'

I hear Dad's voice booming out from the front door and I rush out of my bedroom to meet them. I'm wearing red and gold sari material that Mum's tied into a sarong for me, and white tights with red polka dots, and my special white patent sandals. I know Maya'll like it. It's the kind of thing she might wear.

'Never mind that,' Maya says, 'who's this?'

'It's me,' I say. I know she's joking and feel a bit embarrassed, but pleased too. She says I look gorgeous.

'This is Thomas, by the way,' she says, walking into the living room.

The man behind her raises his hand and says, 'All right there.' He has a big woolly jumper on that must be really hot. I don't think he's handsome enough for Maya. There's something dispirited about him, as if he's making no effort with his face muscles.

In the sitting room Maya puts her hand up the back of Thomas's jumper, and Dad goes into the kitchen to make drinks.

'How're you Maya?' Mum says. She's sitting in the armchair beside the window, and I think she looks beautiful. Her hair, which she normally keeps tied back, streams down her back. She's also put on lipstick and eyeliner, and is wearing my favourite top of hers, the one with flowers and butterflies embroidered round the neck, spangled with tiny mirrors.

'So-so,' says Maya, sounding bored. 'How are you? How're the old biddies?'

'Yeah, okay,' says Mum.

Dad comes through from the kitchen carrying four glasses cupped between his hands. 'An art degree and she ends up cleaning old people's piss,' he says.

He's larger than everyone else in the room, and carries it well, at ease with taking up so much space, unashamed.

Mum laughs, although Maya says it's better than nothing. 'At least there's one gainfully employed person in the house. Better than Brutus here,' Maya says, looking at Dad. 'I don't know how you put up with him, Ann.'

'Oh, he's okay really,' says Mum.

'She hits the bottle,' says Dad. 'That's how she copes with everything.'

Mum sits up angrily and says, 'I do not! Why do you say these things in front of people?'

She jumps up and rushes into the kitchen. After a few minutes Maya says, 'Well done, Richard.'

'Well, it's true,' says Dad, smiling. The long hairs on his arm gleam as if the sun's shining on them.

'You need a good slap,' Maya says, and Dad says he quite possibly does.

Mum comes back from the kitchen, flushed, carrying plates of food. I pass them around, but only Thomas, Dad and I take anything. Mum and Maya continue smoking.

'Oh, the present,' says Maya. 'I'd forgotten.'

Dad opens it slowly and starts saying how nice it is before any of us can see it. I go over and pull apart the wrapping.

'Thomas made it himself,' says Maya.

It's a dulled bronze disc with bars of silver criss-crossing over each other to make a star, and a piece of leather so he can wear it round his neck.

'Put it on, Dad,' I say.

Maya says he's lucky because usually, when she doesn't like someone, she breaks their present before wrapping it, and then pretends it got damaged en route to them.

'But that thing's indestructible,' she says. 'I couldn't break it if I tried.'

'You don't, do you?' says Mum.

'Of course, why would I say it otherwise?'

Dad says she's charming and that he might have to give her a hug. He shakes Thomas's hand, who says, 'No bother, man,' and hugs Maya.

'And my lovely wife,' he says.

He gives Mum a bigger hug that covers her whole body, and kisses her for ages while we watch.

'Stop your nonsense,' Mum says, but she looks pleased.

'Let's have a kissathon,' says Maya flatly, and she kisses Thomas for even longer than Dad kissed Mum. Dad goes into the kitchen and gets everyone another drink. I get a Coke.

'A toast.'

Everyone lifts their glasses.

'To the last hobos,' says Dad.

'The last hobos,' everyone says.

I go round everyone and make them clink their glass with mine.

Guidance

Carrie is my little sister and she's frightened of mostly everything. At night she gets bad dreams about burglars and fires and floods, and us being stuck in the house, not being able to get out. Every night Mum takes us round the windows, and to the door, showing us how tight they're shut. Mum says if there was a flood an aeroplane would pick us up, but it'd have to be a huge flood for that to happen. I tell Carrie not to worry because water goes down, not up. We've flooded Miss Carole downstairs twice now, and she won't say good morning to Mum because of it.

I'm scared of strangers, but not fires or floods or burglars. Everyone knows about fires and floods, but they don't know about strangers. Strangers can look like anyone, and they lure children to go with them, or just grab them, and then they kill them. We watch a cartoon about it in school. A man goes up to a boy in the park and asks him if he wants to go and see his rabbits. When the boy says no, the man offers him a sweet, and then the boy says no again and runs away. Then an adult voice comes over saying, 'Always Say No To Strangers.' After watching this I can't concentrate for thinking what would've happened if the boy had gone with the stranger. And even if the boy ran away from the stranger, the stranger could still run after him and catch him. They don't show you that, but it could happen. When I see men standing near me I wonder if they're strangers, and get ready to run if they talk to me. Men you know aren't strangers, and neither are men at church or policemen. Other than that you can't tell. It seems to me that the best thing to do is to stay at home where I can play with Carrie, and paint, and roller-skate across the kitchen. It's a shame for some kids, like Gail upstairs, who're forced to go out to play. Her skin's a kind of yellowy colour, and Mum says that's because her mum just gives her banana sandwiches every night because she can't be bothered.

Mum says we shouldn't be scared of anything because God is looking after us. She says we're lucky to have God's guidance. She had to be drowning before she saw Him. She says that after Polly, our little sister, died, she wouldn't have been able to carry on without the strength and love He gave her. Sometimes Mum cries about Polly, but she knows she's in heaven and that the Lord chose to take her. Dad never cries and Mum says that's because he's got no feelings, we should pray for him. Dad lies in bed a lot, in the dark, but he doesn't sleep. Once Mum got the minister, Mr Thompson, round to talk to him. Dad just laughed and told the minister he wasn't required, he was wasting his time. It was really embarrassing for us the next day at church. Dad calls Mr Thompson Mum's fancy man, and that makes Mum really angry. She says he saved her life. If she can organize a few meetings or clean the church or make him a nice casserole, then it's the least she can do. Dad says the minister's got plenty of other lady minions, Mum needn't think she's special, and Mum says Dad should shut up, he's got a dirty and diseased mind.

Dad can say very sacrilegious things, and he smokes and drinks. He says Mum used to like a drink too, and that she smoked, but Mum says that's a lie. She says he lost his arm as punishment for The Other Woman. It was sent by God, and that should warn him. Even though it was the leather-cutting machine at his work, Providence was behind it. Dad says Mum fills our heads with rubbish. He can take his plastic arm off and sometimes he waves it at us and chases us round the house. He can be really funny and nice and it makes me sad that he refuses to hear the Word, and won't be able to go to heaven with us.

Carrie has bad dreams which make her scream and cry at night, waking me up. We go through to Mum and beg her to let us stay up. Sometimes it's past eleven o'clock, but Mum makes us hot chocolate and we sit in the living room with her. I watch the clock and think how lovely and late it is. The entire world is asleep but us. The night has a different sound to the daytime, a kind of hum that gets inside my ears, and is all around. Funny noises come from other bits of the house and Carrie says, 'What's that?' and looks scared. Mum tells us that the house gets cold at night and the coldness makes the floorboards creak, and that the fridge always makes funny noises, you just hear them more at night. I know Carrie thinks it's a robber. To impress her I go round all the rooms shouting for the robbers to come out, come out, and it makes me feel better once I know, for sure, that there really is no one there. When I come back I look over at Mum and try to catch her eye. I smile a smile that only she and I will understand. But then Carrie starts snivelling – sometimes she does it on purpose – and Mum just ignores me. She tells Carrie that if there were robbers, she'd sort them out. When thieves broke into Great-granny's house, Great-granny was in bed peeling grapes, and all Great-granny had to do was wave her walking stick at them and the robbers ran out screaming. Carrie can be so stupid, and Mum gives her more attention for being stupid than she gives me for not being stupid.

'Sometimes, Carrie,' I say, 'you're as thick as a plank,' and before I even lean back on the couch, Mum jumps up and slaps me on the leg. It stings like fire and I pull up my pyjama leg to have a look at the mark. I feel more upset the redder it gets. I hope it never goes away and Mum'll have to look at what she's done every day.

'Don't talk to your sister like that,' she says.

She says that I, of all people, should show a bit of compassion, so I say, 'Sorry Carrie.'

'Please don't fight,' says Carrie, and puts her arm through Mum's. 'Tell us a story,' she says.

Mum's favourite is the Good Samaritan, but it makes me feel worse afterwards. In bed I remember the badness of the robbers, not the kindness of the Samaritan. The robbers kick and beat a poor man for nothing and then lots of people come by and don't help. The Good Samaritan walking by was a one in a million chance. A lot of the Bible stories are hard to understand, like the Prodigal Son. I always feel sorry for the other brother; if I was him I wouldn't have eaten that fattened calf, although I don't tell Mum that. But then I try to think it over because the Bible is God's word and He is never wrong, so there must be a message I'm not getting.

Blasphemy is the worst sin. Mum says you should never take God's name in vain, but people do, all the time, even people that go to church. Once, at Brownie Camp, Carrie took God's name in vain. It was because Muriel Dickson was there and Carrie wanted to look smart. And then afterwards, when we were alone, she denied it. I told her lying, as well as blasphemy, was a sin, and then she started crying and admitted it. Since Mum wasn't there to tell her off, I had to be mad and strict with her, and I wouldn't talk to her for five minutes. I promised I wouldn't tell Mum if she prayed for forgiveness, and Carrie said she would, she hated me being mad with her. And so we whispered the Lord's prayer together. I was careful not to say 'hallowed be my name', which is easy to do but still a sin. Carrie said she loved Polly, but that Polly was only a few weeks old, and she loved me more. She loved me more than anything and I loved her more than anything. I said that if she wasn't my sister, and was a boy, I'd marry her when I was older so we could always be together, and Carrie said the same about me.

Our Sunday School is near our house. It's made of reddish-orange bricks which look like bourbon creams joined together with butter icing. Sometimes we have to go to the big church first. I hate that. I can't make any noise or Mum gives me a look. There's a lot of old ladies in our church and a lot of them wear funny bright hats which I can't see past, and I have to just sit there and listen to Mr Thompson's voice. Mr Thompson is huge and thin like a matchstick. When he leans over the pulpit only the top half of his body moves. He always starts by welcoming everyone. He booms out that some of the people gathered before him he knows very well, some are new, and some he's not seen for a while.

'Welcome all,' he says. 'Let's join together in praise.'

I think it would be awful to be one of those people he recognizes as not seeing for a while. They're the people who only come when it suits them, like Miss Wallace, although Mum says she finds the time to attend all the social events going.

The prayers in the big church go on and on. Sometimes I open my eyes, just quickly, and see other people with their eyes open too, and once even a lady picking her nose. Carrie does a great impression of Mr John, the junior minister, saying the prayers. She speaks in the same boring tone as he does, saying, 'And we thank you, Lord, for the tiny petals on the flowers, and the drops of dew on those fragile petals. And we thank you, Lord, for the little bees that feed off those flowers, and the sweet honey those little bees make . . .' on and on and on, just like Mr John. I look sideways at Mum and she's laughing so it must be okay, and so I laugh too. Mum says his preaching's not a patch on Mr Thompson's, and that he's got a way to go yet.

In Sunday School, we first give praise in song. Mrs Tarrant plays the keyboard, hitting the keys with her middle finger and rocking back and forth as if she's possessed. Mum says Mrs Tarrant only got the Sunday School so Mr Thompson could get her out from under his feet. I like the songs with actions in them, songs like 'I Like Jesus Better Than Ice-cream', and I hate the songs where you have to spell things out like J-E-S-U-S. I always say the wrong letter at the wrong time and can't concentrate on singing my praises as I should. After that we go into groups. Carrie has Mr Pickle, and I've got Mrs Proudfoot. Mrs Proudfoot's really tall and fat. She has long arms like paddles that she waves in the air every time anyone sings Hosanna. Sometimes you think she's hurt herself, but she hasn't, she's got the spirit in her.

She says that today we're going to talk about giving our hearts to Jesus. She says that all committed Christians have to do this and those who don't can't get into heaven. She says we have to spread the word so everyone can get into heaven. I put my hand up and say that my dad's a heathen, is there anything I can do? Mrs Proudfoot says I should pray for him, and talk to him, telling him about Jesus' message. She says we should all be out there telling our friends and family and classmates about Jesus. I put my hand up again and say we've tried everything but Dad keeps desisting. It's a good word. I've been waiting all week to use it. It's what Dad says. I lean confidentially into Mrs Proudfoot and say, 'Mum's at her wit's end. He won't do anything but desist.'

Dad came to our church once. Halfway through the sermon, when Mr Thompson asked the Sunday School who their favourite disciples were, Dad put up his hand and said he liked Doubting Thomas best. Mum said she was mortified, and so was I. On the way home they had a terrible argument. Dad said he'd never heard such piffle. He said the God Squad must have brainwashed her, and Mum said one hair on Mr Thompson's head was worth more than the whole lot of him. Me and Carrie hate it when they argue. We lagged behind them and to make us feel happier we started whispering the word piffle to each other. *See that car over there, it's a load of piffle; that's a piffling lovely jacket you're wearing today*, and we started laughing and reminded each other that we'd always have each other.

Mrs Proudfoot hands us out slips of paper with lines typewritten on them. The top line says: Jesus, I give my heart to you, and then there's a gap where you've to sign your name and print the time and date. She says we've to take them home and think before we sign them. It's a serious decision, she says. She says that from that moment on, Jesus is our leader, and as Jesus' foot soldiers our way of life will be hard, but good. The only good way of life.

'I remember the first time I gave my heart to Jesus,' she says, 'and it was a glorious, glorious moment.'

She tells us it was when she was walking through Queen's Park one night.

'It was really dark,' she says, 'and I was scared on account of a man loitering behind me. So I was walking fast and my heart was beating and I was saying to myself, "You're in for it now, Mabel Proudfoot," and then I saw a patch of bright yellow daffodils, shining through the dark.'

She says that was when she knew God would save her from anything. She knew then that He was watching over her and that He wouldn't let anything bad happen to her, and she wasn't afraid any more. She gave Him her heart, there and then, and it was wonderful because she knew that she'd always be safe.

I put up my hand and Mrs Proudfoot sees me but pretends she doesn't. She says that another wonderful thing happened that night. She says she spoke to the man loitering behind her. She told him that Jesus loved him, and he drank up those words like a thirsty man. It turned out he had a lot of troubles and he was going to do something drastic that very night, before he heard those words. Then she says, 'Yes, Amelia, what is it?'

'Actually,' I say, 'I've already given my heart to Jesus.'

Mrs Proudfoot bends over to me right away, smiling. She asks me if I'd like to share that moment.

'It was Christmas Eve,' I start off. 'I was in bed waiting up for Santa . . .'

'Yes?'

'And then, I just did it,' I say. For a moment I'm lost for words. 'I felt His presence in the room,' I say. 'It was as if He was asking me to.'

Mrs Proudfoot asks me if I saw anything, and I say no, I just felt a light.

'That's extraordinary,' she says. 'Did He say anything?' and I say no, it was just the light I felt. The next day, I tell her, Mum found a big bit of glass in her turkey just before she put it in her mouth, and when we told Iceland about it they gave us eight hundred pounds and we all felt sure that was a sign from Him.

Mrs Proudfoot says that's a wonderful story, and how romantic on Christmas Eve. She asks me if she can share it with the rest of the Sunday School and I say I'd rather she didn't, it was between me and Jesus. Then I tell her that I've just remembered that Jesus did speak to me. He said, 'The Lord is my shepherd, I shall not want.'

Ellen puts up her hand and says, 'I've given my heart too, but on New Year's Eve, just before the bells.'

'You have not,' I say, turning round to face her. 'You're making that up.'

'I have so,' she says.

'You have not, Ellen Black, you're copying me.'

Mrs Proudfoot tells us not to argue, and then Jimmy claps his hands at the front of the hall and we all have to go down to listen to the main story. My joy at having Mrs Proudfoot believe me is spoiled a bit, but then I start thinking it over again, and seeing her face all admiring, and thinking how she might take some of the church elders aside, privately, and tell them to look out for me. I decide that me and Carrie will give our hearts to Jesus tonight, on the stroke of midnight.

Jimmy is married to Mrs Proudfoot and is the head of the Sunday School. He looks like a disciple. He's got a beard and long hair. Also, he only wears white clothes and sandals, even in winter. Last week I told Carrie to look at his toes, they look like cashew nuts, and she thought that was funny. She says I'll probably be a dictionary maker when I grow up because I know good words, and I say I might be one of them if I'm not a missionary or the presenter of *Art Attack*.

I go to sit beside Carrie on the floor. Dust floats up my nose and makes me want to scratch it off. I want to tell her about the story I told Mrs Proudfoot, but then Jimmy starts talking. He's talking about the devil, and the temptations the devil can offer. He asks us what we think the devil looks like.

'Do you think he's all in red with two little horns and a pitchfork?' he asks. When Jimmy speaks no one ever talks and no one ever answers his questions. I don't know why, but no one ever does, and I never would. Once James Shearer kept making farting noises while Jimmy was at the blackboard and Jimmy flung a bit of chalk at his head, just suddenly, without saying anything.

'The evil thing about the devil,' he goes on, 'is that he's full of tricks. He can be anyone and anywhere,' he says, putting his hands on his knees. 'Your schoolteacher could be the devil. You could be having a picnic in a field, and a sheep is nibbling the grass beside you.' He pauses, looking round at us. 'That sheep could be the devil,' he says. 'That sheep could turn into the devil and eat you up . . . I could be the devil.'

He asks us how anyone knows he's not the devil.

'Craig,' he says. 'How do you know?'

Craig has orange hair and freckles so close together his face looks made of brown splodges with little bits of skin underneath. He looks at Jimmy with his mouth open and then says, 'Because you're a Christian, sir.'

'Good boy. But guess what, the devil tries even harder with Christians because he's against God and he hates the people who follow Him and what He stands for.'

Jimmy says we have to try even harder than ordinary people. Carrie puts her hand in mine, just quietly, so no one will see. I know she's scared because she was scared by *The Witches*, and that was about schoolteachers who were witches when they took off their make-up and wigs, and they had big scabs on their heads and evil faces. Carrie asked Mum to hide the book from her until she was older.

After the story I go down to the toilet. I want Carrie to come with me, but she won't. I've got to be really desperate to go to the Sunday School toilets. You have to go down a flight of stairs, and then down a corridor with no lights. The corridor smells of pink soap and as you go down it all the noises in the hall disappear and you can only hear yourself walking. There's a side door just beside the toilets and a stranger could just walk in there and no one would hear. I go into the first cubicle and pee really quickly. As I'm washing my hands, Jimmy comes in. I'm about to say hello, but I don't. He comes straight over and stands beside me. He puts his hand up my skirt and inside my knickers and he starts to make noises. I stand very still. It's important I stand very still and don't move. He makes noises like an animal, I don't know why, maybe something's wrong with him. It's like he's turned into something not like a human being. It hurts, and I'm frightened, but I don't say anything. I listen to his noises, and the toilets dripping behind me. I know people shouldn't touch those places. Mum's told me. I know something bad's happening. Then, suddenly, he makes one big noise, and then takes his hand away. He goes over to the sink and washes his hands, looking at his watch. He says, 'Go back now.'

I run all the way, feeling my heart beating and beating. Inside the hall everything looks the same and no one knows what's happened. I go over to get my biscuit but Mr Pickle, who's in charge of the custard creams, says, 'You've had one, don't be greedy,' so I walk over to Carrie who's sitting by herself on the bench.

'It's not fair,' I say, 'Mr Pickle thought I was you and wouldn't give me a biscuit.'

Carrie says I can have a bite of hers, but not too big a bite. She says wasn't that scary about the devil, and I say yeah.

'Do you think it's true?' I say, and Carrie says she doesn't know, it must be.

Kenny

enny told her last week that sometimes he forgot they weren't living together any more. Sometimes, he said, he would turn to say something to her, or switch off the telly and reach for her. It would take him a few moments to realize she wasn't there.

'Our home used to be my sanctuary,' he said. 'Not any more.'

He looked at her face for a response, and June looked away. She concentrated on a patch of wallpaper above the radiator, cream with tiny gold Chinese symbols spread along it. They were probably Chinese for Peace or Love or something. The wallpaper was torn away at one edge, and underneath someone had drawn a willy, resplendent with pubic hair.

'June,' he said, 'd'you hear me?'

'I hear you.'

He sighed and turned away. He wasn't in the habit of being serious or articulating his feelings, and it embarrassed him.

'I don't care what's wrong with you,' he said, 'you'll do for me, June.'

It seemed to June that there'd been a kind of profound silence inside her, for the past few weeks now, and she didn't know if she wanted, or even if she was able, to break it. She supposed she was depressed. She had thought, in a vague, unfocused way, that moving away might help, but nothing had changed. She was still the same.

This morning she wakes early. She lies still, looking out of the window, the sky heaped blue upon blue. A car horn beeps outside and then it's quiet except for the clock ticking. The clock ticking seems to deepen the silence. Mornings are the worst time for her. She tried to describe it to Kenny once, how what she felt, just after waking, was like grief. It was like being overcome with grief, although she didn't know what for.

'I don't understand,' he'd said. 'I don't know what you're talking about.'

'It's like being neither dead nor alive,' she said another time, and Kenny took that as an insult and reminded her of all she had to be happy about.

She gets up and walks to the kitchen, drinks a glass of water, then another one. Things used to be different; she can still remember when things were different. Remembers Kenny, up at six in the morning getting ready for work while she drifted in and out of sleep. The noise of the bathroom taps running, Kenny spitting out toothpaste and washing his face. He's very thorough when it comes to his oral hygiene, hates people with bad breath and embarrassed by the state of his own teeth. He told her once that he used to try not to smile because of them. June was surprised; she hadn't imagined he felt self-conscious about a single aspect of himself.

'They're the only charmless thing about me,' he'd said, nibbling her shoulder, 'so I can't be doing that badly.'

And then, still naked, coming into the bedroom, by the mirror, combing his hair. Him coming over to her, his face, smelling of soap, on her neck, saying, 'Aren't I a handsome devil?' and her laughing. Telling him he looked alarming, telling him to let her sleep.

'Come on, Boo, refresh me,' he'd say, and he'd make her sit up and talk to him.

He called her Boo because when they first met she was too shy to speak to him. He was staying in the hotel she was working in, doing some building work on the west wing extension. One night there'd been a party in the hotel bar and Kenny had come over and spoken to her. He asked her why she never said hello to him, and June said she did say hello to him. She'd blushed and Kenny had said he'd been watching her and he'd decided that she wouldn't say boo to a goose.

They got to know each other over that one summer. On her nights off Kenny took her to expensive restaurants, the funfair on the other side of Ayr pier, to the ten-pin bowling and the cinema. He was earning a lot from the hotel job and was angry if she tried to pay for anything. It violated his sense of what it was to be a man. Also, he liked to spend money, and liked other people knowing he spent money. One night, walking along the beach in the rain, he asked her how much she thought his socks cost.

'Have a look,' he said and lifted up his trouser leg. 'How much?'

June said she didn't know, two pairs for a fiver? Kenny roared with laughter. He said they were Armani, fifteen pounds a pop. She'd been horrified.

'Aren't you ashamed,' she said, 'of spending that kind of money on socks?'

'Ashamed? Why should I be ashamed? I left school a dunderhead with one standard grade, and now I'm wearing Armani socks. Why should I be ashamed?' He put his arm around her and said, 'I'm still a dunderhead right enough, but we all have our crosses to bear.'

Kenny liked to turn everything into a party. He knew how to tell a story, gleefully, how to make his digressions more interesting than his original story. He dealt efficiently with interruptions, knowing when it was best to hand the floor over to someone else, and when to dismiss them. And though he never laughed at his own jokes, there was always this feeling that he was deliberately reining himself in, that he wouldn't be able to stop laughing if he started. Kenny was funny. Instinctively he understood the comic value of certain words, words that other people knew but never used. He made everyone sound ridiculous, but lovably so. Regularly, at the end of the night, June would be sitting, quiet, surrounded by a bunch of people she barely knew. Kenny would be holding court, getting higher and higher, making everyone laugh. At two or three or four in the morning, in that dismal Royale Hotel bar, Kenny'd leap up and fetch the night watchman, Mr Henry, to their table. June was frightened of Mr Henry. He seemed ancient, his face lean and ferocious, dark brown and creviced from the sun. He'd once accused June of stealing a fibreglass maid that stood at the door of the hotel.

'Right, what is it?' Mr Henry would say. Kenny would point at June and shout that they couldn't shut her up. She hadn't taken her medication, he'd shout, she was a troublemaker, and they wanted her thrown out. Everyone would scream with laughter, and Mr Henry would be furious, telling Kenny he'd no time for his tomfoolery.

'But you're laughing inside,' Kenny would say, slinging his arm over Mr Henry's shoulder.

After breakfast she cleaned the rooms on the top floor where Kenny and his workmates were staying. He would take his break at eleven and meet her up there. They would sit on the edge of the hard bed eating the complimentary shortcake and watching *Colombo*. They didn't talk much when they were alone. One morning he said he thought they should take their clothes off.

'You can keep your hat on,' he said.

'Thank goodness for that,' said June.

'If you think I'm the kind of guy who would put a girl's modesty in jeopardy,' said Kenny, 'then think again.'

Light came through the cheap blue curtains, the bed sheets hadn't been changed yet, and June could feel the grit which Kenny trailed with him from work press into her back. Afterwards he put his arm behind her neck and kissed her face.

'I didn't know you'd never, you know, done the deed,' he said.

'Well, I didn't tell you.'

'Was it okay? I didn't hurt you?'

'It was okay. I wanted to.'

They lay in silence, and after a while June said, 'You look sad.'

Sometimes she thought she could sense a sort of sadness from him. It was his eyes, she'd decided. They were pale, luminous blue, dark-lashed, and sometimes, seeing him by the door, or alone in repose, they had a dignified, sober melancholy about them.

'I am sad,' said Kenny, 'I've just missed the *Colombo* double bill.'

'Seriously,' she said, laughing. 'Aren't you ever sad?'

Kenny scrunched up his face meditatively and said, 'Do you remember when Jamie died in *EastEnders*? On Christmas fucking Eve, when Sonia was waiting for him, when he'd just bought her an engagement ring? He was all happy and excited and then that bastard Martin Fowler had to run him over. There was a definite lump in my throat that night.'

She laughed, and Kenny kissed her cheek and said, 'Why would I ever be sad? Not one bad thing's ever happened to me in my whole life.'

June said, 'It must be terrible to have a happy childhood. It doesn't prepare you for all the crap to come. I'm glad,' she said, 'that I'd such a bad one.'

'How was it so bad?'

'You tell me about yours first.'

Kenny shrugged and said there was nothing to tell. It was just happy.

'Tell me one thing you remember,' she said, 'anything at all.'

Kenny paused and then smiled. 'There was this one time in primary school,' he said. 'We had to draw pictures of Britain during the war. So I drew a wee boy with a banana skin in his hand and a big smile and one of those bubbles coming out his mouth saying YUM. And then the teacher comes round to look at all our drawings, and everyone else's drawn unhappy people and rubbly buildings and stuff. So she comes to mine and looks at it and says, "What's that?" and points to the banana skin. And I say, "A banana skin," and she goes, "But there weren't any bananas during the war," and I say, "That's why the boy's so happy. 'Cause he's found a banana." There,' Kenny said, 'will that do?'

'Yes,' she said, laughing, 'that'll do.'

*

June goes into the bedroom to wake Billy. He's lying with his eyes open and starts smiling when she bends down to him. He's got blue eyes and dark hair, like Kenny, and also Kenny's sunny disposition. He looks around as if he's willing the world to delight him. When he was first born, June was scared of holding him. What if she tripped, what if she dropped him? He was as breakable, as miraculous, as an eggshell, while around her the world of things had taken on a frightening solidity – the world of uncovered sockets, matches, stairs, and cookers. If you were vigilant you could guard against the danger of things, although not against cot death, measles, whooping cough. She read handbooks, memorized symptoms; Kenny got annoyed and said she was morbid. She read a story in a magazine about a woman who'd mistakenly put her baby in the microwave when she was in a psychotic trance.

'That's enough, June,' Kenny had said when she told him about it. 'If you want to scare yourself, read a horror book.'

Sometimes, watching Kenny sling Billy over his shoulder, she was envious of how easily everything came to him. He didn't think about the precariousness of life, it didn't terrify him the way it terrified her. His love for Billy, and for her too, is unsparing, without anxiety. This is the way, she thinks, that he will love whoever he chooses to love.

She dresses Billy and feeds him porridge in the kitchen. He's getting bigger and more substantial every day – Billy Bunting, Kenny calls him – his skin soft, and fine as icing sugar, tender rolls of fat under his chin, over his knees and wrists. She lifts up his legs and kisses his feet. One day, she realizes, she won't be able to do this any more, and a terrible feeling of loss comes over her. It's not an unwelcome feeling; she's glad to feel anything. There've been days recently when she thinks that someone could drive a nail through her arm and she wouldn't even blink. She lifts Billy from his highchair and carries him round the kitchen. There's a mouldy cauliflower in the fridge, and hardly anything else. She finished the milk this morning, and there's no washing powder left. She takes out the cauliflower and puts it down on the counter, staring at it, wondering what to do next. The more she stares at the cauliflower, the more unrecognizable it becomes, the more incomprehensible. When Billy starts to wriggle, she shakes herself and throws it in the bin.

The dishes need washing, clothes need washing, she needs to buy food. If she'd bothered to get the phone connected, she could ring Kenny and ask him to bring some stuff over tonight when he picks up Billy. She could go to the shops herself, but the thought fills her with dread and she pushes it out of her mind.

She's been living here two months now. It was the first flat the council offered her, and the man who showed her round asked her if she was sure she didn't want to wait for something better to come up. No, she said, it was fine. She didn't care where she lived as long as it was away from where she'd been. She would have gone anywhere. So she found herself here, in a high-rise, nine stories above the ground. There's a lift, but it's usually broken, and she doesn't like it anyway. It's claustrophobic and airless, full of the breath and germs of everyone who's been inside it. The stairs are just as bad, dark, smelling of urine. If you tripped and fell down the stairs you would die, and when June is on the stairs she thinks about this, and starts forgetting how to walk at all. One day last week she'd stopped on the eighth landing, Billy in her arms, too frightened to go any further.

She turns on *Sesame Street* and sits Billy on her knee. They play a game where June pretends to disappear, dropping her face behind her hand and counting one, two, three. Billy looks at her with his big serious eyes, laughing hysterically when she pops her face up over her hands. She blows raspberries onto his stomach, and then gets out his books to read. He can't talk yet, although she and Kenny used to try to decipher his gurgles, re-forming and shaping them into English. They were confident that he was going to be a genius. The book she's reading him today is about a little girl walking down a street, naming all the objects she passes. June points to the pictures and reads out the words underneath –

mummy, tree, cherry, dog – until she can no longer make sense of what she's saying, pure meaningless sounds coming out of her mouth. Billy touches her lips with his fingers; he knows he's losing her. Soon he gets sleepy, and she puts him back in his cot for a nap.

She worries that she's becoming a capricious mother. Some days she'll play with Billy for hours and hours, desperately using her energy to think up new games for him. It's Billy who eventually crawls away to play by himself. Other days she can hardly be bothered to talk to him. This upsets her because, above all, she wants to be a good mum. She doesn't want Billy to go through what she went through. The days when her mother would lie in bed, tears falling silently down her face. Once June wiped her cheeks and her mother had looked up at her blankly, as if she didn't recognize her. Her Aunt Helen used to come over to clean the house and make dinner, wash her school uniform. She told June one night that her mother was ill, but that it didn't mean she didn't love her. The same night, getting out of bed for a glass of water, June overheard them talking in the kitchen.

'You have options, Elizabeth,' she heard Helen say. 'I know you don't think so, but you do.'

Her mother didn't reply.

'June could come and live with me,' said her aunt.

'I couldn't do that,' said her mum.

'You could go into hospital, get some proper medical help. See a psychiatrist.'

'I couldn't do that.'

Her aunt went on and on, until at last June heard her say, 'You don't want to die. No one wants to die.'

When her mother didn't respond, June froze. It felt as if the whole world had suddenly been stilled.

'There,' said Helen, 'that's lots of options. Let's go through them again.'

And June had stood in the hall in her nightdress, her heart thumping, listening to them haggle over her mother's life.

*

She goes back into the kitchen, at a loss what to do first. She starts running water for the dishes although when the basin's full she turns off the tap and looks out of the window instead. She can see the Fancy Café, where she went once for a cup of tea, the waitresses cooing over Billy; and Corinne's Hair, and Rajou's with an iron grille over the cash desk. On the other side of the road is Pollokmews train station, looking surprisingly quaint and rural amidst all the graffiti and junk and concrete ugliness of the rest of the area. At first she thought it'd be good living somewhere where everything was so close together. It'd be easier, she'd thought, to manage herself here. But it's not turned out that way: she's spent more time looking out of the window than she's spent outside. The things she sees from the window have taken on a nebulous, impalpable quality, as if they exist in a film or a dream. She finds herself concentrating on one thing at a time – a woman's hands moving, her feet, her face – unable to merge the features together to make a whole living person.

Today she looks towards the train station, watches a bald man lurch like a sleepwalker down the platform. He's got a plastic Somerfield bag round his arm; it swings as it blows in the wind. She turns to look at the clock and when she looks back, he's falling backwards over the edge of the platform. It happens in a second, the movement as neat and final as a domino toppling over. She presses her face to the window but can only see the empty platform. It takes her a few seconds to move, running to Billy's cot, pulling him up, Billy crying. Running to the door, her hands sweating, sweat all over her. Billy screaming in her arms. She's not even out of the front door when she hears the train coming. Running back to the window, she sees it gather speed and roar past the station. Then everything's exactly the same again. The sky arches on.

Inside the flat June screams, and the noise mixes with Billy wailing and a Tina Turner song someone's playing at top volume in the flat below.

*

When Kenny arrives she's sitting with Billy on her lap. He asks what's happened, the door was standing open. He stops and looks at her.

'What's wrong?' he says, coming close and directing her face towards him. 'What's happened?'

'I can't talk just now,' she says.

He asks if it has anything to do with Billy, and she shakes her head. He sits beside her, taking Billy from her arms.

'I think I'll stay,' he says.

When Billy goes back off to sleep, Kenny makes them a coffee. The room gets darker and darker but neither of them switches on the light.

'June,' he says.

She hears it faintly, as if it's coming over great distances to reach her.

'June.'

He kneels down in front of her, and puts his head on her lap, his arms tight around her legs.

'I'm sorry,' he says.

'Please,' she says, putting her hand on his head. 'Shh.'

Voices

John is a sound sleeper. It's a quality Simone envies. She says it points to a rested state of mind. She watches his chest rise and fall. His face is unlined, wide planes of skin over his forehead and across his cheeks. Like a Halloween pumpkin, she used to say to him. *You're like a big, friendly Halloween pumpkin.*

She wrote letters to him when they first started going out. She spent hours thinking them over, writing them out again and again until she had a final draft. Then she would write that one out, messily, as if she'd just dashed it off. She wrote down bits of songs and poems that reminded her of him. Also, things that she thought would amuse or impress him. One of them, she remembers, was a Stevie Smith poem: 'I want to be your pinkie/ I am tender to you/ My heart opens like a cactus flower/ Do you thinky I will do?' She looks back, in wonder that she ever wrote such a thing.

John liked the letters but not as much as she liked writing them. He was still in art school then, and drew her a few pictures back as an exchange. He liked drawing very detailed ink cartoons, cramming as many people as he could onto the page. (He used to say he failed his degree because his drawings were too cheerful. Every time he handed in work his tutor would roll his eyes and say, 'Another fucking smorgasbord of fun.') Once Simone said he'd to write something personal on the next drawing he gave her, a dedication. A week later he handed her a picture of a party – it was the party they had first met at – with *I saw you across the room: your eyes were the colour of turds* written at the top. John thought it was hilarious, but Simone didn't.

Recently she's been thinking about those letters. It must have been seven years ago she wrote them, although it seems much, much longer. It seems a lifetime away. She wanted to see them again, but when she asked John if he still had them, he couldn't remember.

'What kind of human being throws away love letters?' she'd said. John had laughed and said they weren't love letters, they were just her way of showing off her plumage. But they had found them. They were tucked away in a big box of receipts and bills and documents that they had carried from flat to flat, and never looked in. There were only four letters. Simone was sure, at first, that there must have been more. Then, when she thought about it, four was about right. Four letters over about six months. She was disappointed, although she didn't know why.

The alarm shows eight thirteen. John's arm is round her waist and she tries not to move. It's nice to lie like that for a while. When John wakes up she tells him about the dream she had.

'It was so strange,' she says. 'I was boxed into the corner of this empty room. It was a beige colour, and there was a fridge there but nothing else. So I was backed up against the wall, terrified because someone was trying to hurt me. I was endangered. And then I saw it was you. It was you that was trying to hurt me. And I kept screaming at you to stop, but you wouldn't. I was sweating when I woke up.'

'That's a funny word to use,' says John. '*Endangered*.'

Other people's dreams bore him. When they were first married Simone would tell him her dreams every night, the comical and bizarre and wretched universes she had travailed in her sleep. He suspected her of making them up.

'Don't you think that's odd though, to dream something like that?'

She's sitting up now, staring at the wall opposite and not really talking to John at all. He's drifting back to sleep. When she gets up he rolls over and curls his body over the expanse of the bed like he's been waiting all the time for it to be vacated.

In the kitchen she makes a cup of tea and drinks it standing by the window. The sun is shining into the back green. Outside everything is absolutely still, stalled under its glare. The office has been terrible, no air-conditioning, everyone hot and irritable. Everyone except for Lloyd, who doesn't seem to get irritated about anything. He's still wearing his heavy suit, waistcoat, bow tie. Trussed up like a Christmas turkey when all the other men are in short sleeves.

'He looks like a character in a Dickens novel,' she told John once. 'One of the fat, sweaty, insufferably jolly ones. And he doesn't even realize, he doesn't realize how odd he looks.'

John isn't much interested in Dickens or Lloyd. 'Fair play to him,' he'd said. 'He gets your vote.'

Lloyd started working with them five months ago. There are only four of them in the office – her and Lisa who do the admin work; Bob who manages the finances, and now Lloyd, ostensibly their boss. His job is to visit the people on social security who've put in claims for free cookers or washing machines or fridges. He never refuses any of them, which is creating more work for all of them, and causing Bob to be more excessively, abrasively courteous than usual.

'I just don't understand how we can let people live in these conditions,' Lloyd said yesterday. He was sitting on the edge of Simone's desk, wiping his face with a handkerchief. He always comes back from his visits slightly perplexed and saddened, as if he's been personally let down by the system. Simone said it wasn't just that the government *let* them, it was the government that forced them into it.

'Tony Blair doesn't give a fuck about these people,' she said.

'I like Tony Blair,' said Lisa. 'He's got a hard job, I'd like to see you try it.'

Simone ignored her and went back to her computer screen.

Lloyd said he didn't know they had a communist on their hands, and Simone blushed and said she wasn't a communist.

'I'm a socialist,' she said.

'Red under the bed!' roared Lloyd joyously. He got up and paced around the room. 'I'm sweating like nobody's business,' he said, getting out his handkerchief again. Bob had gone for lunch and she and Lisa were typing out letters. After a few minutes he patted his stomach and said he was getting heck of a fat. Lisa didn't look up, but Simone did, and then she had to hear about his weight problem, and the diet Susie, his wife, had put him on, and all the foodstuffs he yearned for, the monumental deprivation involved in not eating them.

She's never experienced anyone who likes to talk as much as Lloyd. If he isn't talking, he looks wounded. He likes talking, especially, about himself. The quirks of his preferences enchant him.

'I can't entertain an onion,' he'll say into the quiet. 'I can't abide pictures not straight,' and he sounds delighted with himself. 'Teeth,' he says, 'aren't they funny when you think of them?'

Simone went home with a headache. John had got off work early on flexi-time, and was watching *Neighbours*.

'Uh oh,' he said when she walked in, 'you've got your disagreeable face on.'

She told him how behind she was with all her paperwork, and how clammy and poky it was in the office.

'It's Saturday tomorrow. Chill out,' he said, which is his solution to all the world's ills. When they first started seeing each other he was fond of saying, after a few drinks, 'I don't know why everyone can't get on and love each other.'

Simone kept complaining. She said how she has to sit in that tiny room all day with Lloyd smoking away until she can't see a thing in front of her. And how every chance he gets he puts his hands on her. One of these days she'll have to say something. He pretends he's a roadrunner and says 'beep beep' and holds her waist, even though she's not blocking his way any.

'D'you want me to beat him up?' John said.

'You've not seen him, he's a big fella,' Simone said. She tucked her feet under John's legs and lay back on the sofa. 'He could probably wrestle a carthorse to the ground,' she said. 'But thanks for having the good grace to be jealous.'

'No problemo,' said John, and switched the channel over to *The Simpsons*.

She finishes her tea and makes another cup for John. He's awake and staring at the ceiling.

'What's this,' she says, 'existential angst?'

'Not likely,' he says. He points to the ceiling. 'That crack's getting bigger,' he says. 'We need to do something about it.'

'It's fine, John.'

She sits on the edge of the bed. 'Do you ever wonder about people in work after you've gone home?' she says. 'I mean, what they do at night or at the weekend? What their homes are like?'

He says he doesn't. 'Categorically no,' he says, 'I never wonder at all.'

'I thought you'd say that,' she says.

'Do you?'

'Of course.'

'I thought you'd say that.'

He turns and smiles without showing his teeth. There's something diffident and lovely about the smile that makes her smile back. They had met at a party. Simone had gone with a girl she didn't know very well. All her other friends had suddenly got boyfriends. The girl – whose name she can't even remember any more – had got wretchedly drunk and insisted on singing interminably long folk songs in the sitting room. Whenever anyone spoke or laughed while she was singing, she gave them a fixed, aggressive stare. At one point she broke off and threatened to hit one of the boys if he didn't shut up. Simone walked through to the kitchen and poured herself a drink. John was leaning against the wall, tall and spare with, Simone noticed, a disproportionately large head to his body. He was smiling agreeably and looking spectacularly uninvolved in what was going on around him. As if he was at home, watching a comic film. She spoke to some people she knew from university, and when she looked back at John he was eating Pringles with dedicated enjoyment. She went over to him and said hello, and he had to chew down his crisps before he said hello back. He held out the tube and offered her one, and Simone said no thanks.

'You know what it's like,' she said. 'Once you pop, you can't stop.'

'Tell me about it,' said John. 'I don't even like Pringles.'

'You look like you're fair enjoying them,' Simone said, and he laughed.

Quite soon after that, they were living together. It seemed to happen without decision, the way tumbleweed rolls aimlessly from one place to the next. Or this is how it appears to her now, looking back. She can still remember every detail of that first flat. How cramped and dark it was, the smell of spoiling meat drifting up from the butcher's below. At night mice would begin to scramble about in the kitchen. John hated them. He had visions of them flinging themselves, kamikaze style, onto his face as he slept. He would climb out of bed and chase them round the kitchen. He only ever caught two. He took them down to the back green and set them free. Simone used to tell their friends this – *And he won't even kill them* – using a tone of gentle exasperation, although secretly she was proud of him. John would smile his what's-a-nice-guy-to-do smile. He liked her telling this story; he liked what it told people about him.

Simone used to say that it was like living in a barnyard, but really she didn't mind. She felt, in some way, that they were living authentically. The broken TV resting on piles of old *Yellow Pages*, the tatty, fawn-coloured wallpaper, the dinners of chicken supreme from a can. They were happy there, although sometimes she realized that one day it would make her unhappy. That one day she would want a bigger flat, a job with prospects, the kind of clean, ample life that she imagined other married people had.

'Will we put the idiot box on?' says John, yawning and stretching his arms. He's uncharacteristically theatrical when it comes to yawns, burps, and sneezes. He puts his whole body into them.

'Just leave it. I hate the drone of it in the morning.'

He gets up to open the window and they talk about what they're going to do today. He suggests the park, but Simone says she's got to choose wallpaper. She'll get more done if he's not there.

'Okey dokey,' he says, getting back into bed. After a few minutes he reaches over and runs his finger along the silver stretch marks on the side of her hip.

'Your skin's always warm,' he says, 'and mine's always cold. You could boil an egg between your hands.'

'Bad circulation,' she says, 'you should get more exercise. You could strip the hall today,' she says, and John says, 'I suppose I could. I don't know if I'm that way inclined,' he says, and Simone says to start inclining.

Simone's gone to his house three weekends in a row now. She doesn't know why and it spoils it if she thinks about it. She doesn't stay long. Last Saturday she just walked down the street and got the bus home. It's a fairly new house, anonymous and unappealing. White pepple-dash on the outside, very neat and angular and serviceable. It looks like a house no one lives in. She had expected something more established, something more abundant. Something more like Lloyd. It doesn't suit him.

Today she opens the gate and goes down the path. The front window's open and a sudden breeze blows a pink gauze curtain in, then out. She crouches down and peers through the gap. She's never been able to look inside before. There's a white wall, and a corner of a mantelpiece with a pair of socks held down by a clock. They look like disembodied limbs. It's not what she had imagined at all. She had imagined a room full of mahogany. Chairs and tables with a shiver of dust along their legs, redolent of a kind of shabby grandeur. She had imagined rosy faded leather and a lamp with tassels, picture frames resting on crocheted doilies. On Saturday mornings Lloyd would get up late and sit here while he had his breakfast. Statesmanlike in a long bathrobe, flip-flop slippers that slapped when he walked. He and Susie would have a fried breakfast. Susie, she imagines, is pink and plump as a Russian doll. Lloyd says skinny women give him the jitters. All those bones, he says. Afterwards he'd have a shower, maybe a bath. He'd talc himself and put pomade in his hair. (She doesn't know what pomade is, but she imagines that's what he'd use. It sounds gentlemanly and clean-smelling.) He'd go into the bedroom, naked and soft, unselfconscious as a baby, and Susie would be sitting by a dressing table putting on make-up and she wouldn't look up. At one they'd leave the house without bustle and get into the car to visit his mother in the nursing home. Simone knows this bit, anyway, is true. He talks about her a lot.

'Mother was even more doolally than usual,' he said once. 'She was accusing me of stealing her forks.'

He never sounds sad when he talks about her and her increasing descent into what he calls pottiness. Maybe they never got on. He always calls her 'Mother', which makes Simone imagine someone brooding and totemic, summed up in one word like Bowie or Madonna.

So, the nursing home. Lloyd would flirt with her, even if she didn't respond. He'd joke about her boyfriend, about all her boyfriends, and he'd shake the old men's hands and call them sir. He'd be his gallant best. He'd compliment the other women on their hair and ask after their health. He'd tell the nurses that they were real sweeties. Everyone would love him. It would be bad faith not to love him when he'd tried so hard, so diligently, to court them.

The whole time Susie would talk to his mother. She'd fuss around making things comfy, pouring tea, offering Jaffa Cakes. For some reason Susie doesn't seem a mystery to Simone. She dismisses her, in a way she can't dismiss Lloyd. She thinks of her as an indisputably nice person, earnest, though not very bright. Not given to flights of fancy, vanity, intimations or introspection. She'd talk to Lloyd's mum in a confidential way. Touch the old woman's arm when she made a joke about Lloyd, or men in general. 'Boys will be boys,' she'd say.

She'd humour Lloyd affectionately, and afterwards he'd say what an angel she was, and how he wouldn't be able to cope without her. 'Oh,' she'd say, not taking much notice, 'I think you'd do fine.'

Simone walks down the path that runs along the side of the house, into the back garden. She's seen it before, found it disappointing in its ordinariness. It was like getting something you already owned for a birthday gift. She felt cheated, which she knew was ridiculous.

There's a border of red and white flowers, wilting under the sun, and a tree beside the gate. The washing line, which was empty two weeks ago, has two white shirts and a bra hanging on it. They're grainy coloured and not very clean. She walks up to the kitchen window. The Venetian blinds are pulled down, and all she can see is her own face reflected back at her. She looks around and doesn't know what to do next. It's an indecently beautiful day, a blue sky spans on and on above her. She realizes she's sweating but she doesn't want to take her coat off. Sitting on the steps leading to the back door she has a sudden urge to laugh.

'Can I help you there?'

Simone turns and sees a woman leaning over next-door's fence. She has a long, bony, tanned face, like a race-dog that's seen better days and is now nursing unspoken, long-term grievances. She also has an Alice band, and a sweater with a white collar and a strip of Disney characters appliquéd across the chest.

'I don't know,' Simone calls back. She gets up and wipes her trousers down. 'Where would be the best place to break in?'

'I beg your pardon?' says the woman, staring at her, and not in a friendly fashion.

Simone apologizes and says she was just joking. She tells the woman she's looking for the Smiths.

'I'd have phoned,' she says, 'but I wanted to surprise them.'

'Oh, that's nice. They're out just now, left about one. They'll probably be back soon.'

'Yes.'

Since the woman keeps standing there, Simone says, 'It's a lovely house. Have you seen what they've done with the sitting room?'

She says she hasn't, she didn't know they were decorating, and Simone says, 'You know what Susie's like. Everything has to be new.'

After a few minutes of uncomfortable silence the woman says, 'Have you known them for long then? Only I've not seen you around before.' She's still looking at Simone suspiciously, as if she's unhygienic.

'Old friends. It's Lloyd I'm really acquainted with,' she says. 'We go way back.' Making a decisive move forward, she says she'll catch them another time. 'No need to tell them I was here,' she says.

And she walks straight down the path, through the gate and down the street without looking back. She feels exhilarated. She feels she's flying, even though she knows she's about to crash to earth any moment.

Over tea they talk about the hall. Simone says she fancies burnt orange, maybe paint instead of wallpaper. She didn't see anything she liked today.

'Whatever,' says John. 'I'll strip it tomorrow, I promise.'

'It's a simple thing to ask, John, that's all I'm asking you to do.'

They sit in the living room and Simone watches telly while he reads the *National Geographic*.

'Look at that,' John says. 'That's what they think Mercury looks like.'

He holds out the page but all Simone can make out is a blur of brown.

'There are no days on Mercury,' he says. 'One side's

perpetually blistered by the sun and the other side's perpetually frozen.'

'That sounds like a poem,' she says. '*There are no days on Mercury.*'

'I've missed my calling.'

'I'd like to be interested in the *National Geographic*,' she says, 'but I'm not. I remember I used to think you knew such a lot, and then I realized you got it from that magazine. You'd tell me something about Sub-Saharan Africa or something and I'd think, "How does he know that? Where does he get this stuff from?"'

'It's been a good friend,' he says, smiling. 'It's got me through some difficult conversations.'

Simone says it's funny how he's interested in facts and she's interested in people.

'Some people,' he says, taking up the magazine and starting to read again.

'What's that supposed to mean?' she says, and he says, nothing. Just that she's interested in some people more than others.

'Like who?'

'I don't know. You tell me.'

He shakes his head and says, 'Come on, let's just have a nice night. Let's not argue, okay?'

'I'm not arguing,' she says, 'I'm just talking.'

She turns back to the telly and he goes into the kitchen.

In bed, he touches her shoulder to pull her towards him. She moves slightly so as not to offend him, and then moves back again. Into the darkness she says, 'I've done something terrible.'

The silence that follows unnerves her. She says, 'Don't you want to know what?'

'No, then I would have to think of you terribly.'

She's so angry she can hardly speak. 'If you cared about me you'd want to know,' she says.

'It's because I care about you I don't want to know.'

In the flat next door dogs start barking wildly, and then they hear a front door close and their neighbours, Carol and Kevin, moving around.

'Those dingoes were going crazy all day,' John says. 'I couldn't hear myself think.'

It's quiet for a few minutes and then they hear Carol shout, 'No, you shut it!' and then Kevin shouting something in reply.

'I don't know why they can't have their skirmishes quietly,' says John, turning over. The dogs start baying again, and Carol threatens to slug Kevin.

'We have to do something about these walls,' John says. 'Insulate them or something. I heard egg boxes are good. We could get them at the fishmonger's. It makes me feel besmirched,' he says, 'having to listen to everything that goes on in there.'

'I like it,' says Simone. 'I like the voices.'

Connections

Me and Brona are walking down the lane home. Sometimes I walk this way to avoid Graeme, and sometimes Brona comes with me. We're listening to her personal stereo, an earphone each. The tape is Lou Reed's *Transformer*. We sing along to 'Take a Walk on the Wild Side'. I ask Brona what song reminds her of me, and she says she doesn't know.

'None of them, really,' she says.

'Well you,' I say, 'you remind me of that song "You're So Vicious".'

'What? *When I see you coming I just want to run. You're not good, and you're certainly not any fun?* That's nice,' she says.

'No, not like that,' I say. 'I mean, it's a compliment. You're just crazy and wild and don't care. It's a compliment. You also remind me of "Take a Walk on the Wild Side",' I say.

Brona's legs are turning blue with the cold. She hoicks up her socks. Nobody wears white knee socks except Brona. She also wears the full school uniform, which no one else does. She says she feels obliged to be different, not to follow the herd. She has a dreamy, blank face which sometimes looks like an artist's muse in days of yore, and sometimes looks like a pornographic model's, the same rapt self-absorption. There is a sharp red birthmark down her right cheek that tails off in little islands down to her chin. The doctor wants to burn it away but Brona won't let him and I say she's right because it's part of her. It's special.

*

Brona has been my best friend for four years, since we were eleven and in first year. I hated school before Brona came. There was a girl called Dione McCurdle, whom I was terrified of. She came up to me on the first day of school and said, 'Are you a gypsy?'

'No,' I said.

'You look like one.'

Her friend laughed, but Dione didn't. There was a peculiar grim strain to her bullying, as if she didn't enjoy it. She stood right in front of me as if she were going to remain there eternally, blocking my way.

'You know what else she looks like,' she said to her friend. 'A munchkin. You know, those fat things with the cheeks.'

Everyone was scared of Dione. She was stolidly fat and white, as if all her flesh was straining against the confines of skin. Once someone's mum went round to her house to complain about her, and Dione's dad punched the woman in the face. She was a fairly democratic bully, and the worst I suffered was a few perfunctory jabs from her compass in maths. At night, though, I would lie awake imagining scenarios in which I would become the sole victim and focus of her attention. I choked back tears of sorrow for my imaginary plight, my littleness, my persecution. But then, after Christmas, Brona started school. Dione hated her. Brona thought she was someone. She answered all the questions in class and sometimes even corrected the teachers. It came to a head one lunchtime when Dione stole Brona's scarf and ran round the playground with it. Finally she dropped it in a puddle and stamped on it whilst looking straight at Brona. Brona charged at her, and people started yelling *Fight*. It only lasted a few minutes, everyone closed in around them. I was at the back and could only hear grunts, a yelp, caught a momentary flash of legs and hair. When they stood up, Dione told Brona to keep her stupid fuckin' scarf. In silence Brona lifted it up and put it round her neck. One end was completely black with mud and dripping wet. She gave it an expressive flick over her shoulder and sauntered off.

After school I followed Brona down the road. I said to her that I loved what she had done.

'Oh, the fight,' she said. 'Oh well.'

'Weren't you scared?'

She said she'd just got that scarf for Christmas. She wasn't about to relinquish it (that was the word she used) to Bully-guts.

'I just really like this scarf,' she said.

She said everyone at her last school thought she was mental. Two girls there had told everyone that she dissected live tadpoles for kicks.

'Did you?' I asked, and Brona said no, but she wasn't going to tell them that.

We reach the end of the lane. Brona says it's disappointing we've still not seen one single flasher here this year. If we do see a flasher, Brona says we've to stand still, point to his todger and laugh. I would never do that, but I say okay.

'Ciao for now,' she says.

'See you,' I say.

There's nothing that depresses me more than walking down my street, Friday afternoon, four o'clock. The flats line up in strict geometry down both sides of the road, the sun shining ruthlessly making everything seem immutable, unchangeable, just there. I will be forever walking down this street with its no shadows, no noise, looking into curtained windows at four o'clock, Friday. I hum Del Amitri, *Nothing ever happens, nothing happens at all.* I see Graeme come out of our close and he sees me and starts coming over.

'You were slow this morning,' he says. 'I waited but I didn't hear you come down the stairs.'

'I dogged registration,' I say. 'Sorry.'

Whenever possible I dog registration so I don't have to walk to school with Graeme. It's not because he's some sort of psychopath or anything. It just depresses me seeing him at his door, his jacket zipped up, ready to go. In the mornings I creep down the stairs as if they're booby-trapped, placing my shoe bit by bit on the steps to minimize noise, my back hunched spy-style.

Once Graeme saw me. I had to straighten up, embarrassed, not knowing what to say. But if Graeme did realize, he didn't care.

'Caught you,' he said, and ambled to my side.

'I hate registration too,' says Graeme. I slow down to keep pace with him. He does everything slowly, as if he has to negotiate the action beforehand, as if he goes through processes. 'It's because of my name,' he says. 'I think they think it's funny.'

'Graeme Gay,' I say. 'It's not the best surname. They're just immature.'

He looks at his feet and smiles. He says he realized something funny in geography today. He realized how many places had the word kill in them.

'*Kil*marnock,' he says, 'East *Kil*bride. *Kil*winning. *Kil*martin. It's frightening.'

'Oh,' I say. 'I've never thought about it like that.' After a bit I say, 'There's *Kil*malcolm too.'

'Yeah, that's another one.'

Mum's in the hall when I get in, painting a table. She's wearing two odd shoes and her paint-splattered trousers with her hair wrapped up in a red scarf.

'What're you defacing now?' I say.

'Look, I picked it up this morning.'

When Mum says she's picked something up it means she's been to the skip again. She says the skip's full of finds, perfectly good things that people just throw out. It mystifies her. We've fought about this, the skip being near school and my horror at the thought of someone seeing her carrying away her loot like a happy dung beetle. Mum says I'm too conservative. She says, with a regal air, that she's an eccentric, and I've not shaken off the feeling that this is a state to aim for. I don't want to be a normal person myself, I just want her to be.

'I'm thinking poetry in the middle here,' she says. 'What d'you think?'

'No. Just no. Leave it the way it is.'

The flat is stuffed with things Mum's customized. This is made worse by the fact that she's a slapdash and indifferent artist. There are birds on our cupboards with bulging turkey bodies and smeared pinhead faces; there are phantasmagorical blue lettuce-head flowers on the kitchen wall, mermaids graffitied round the bathroom mirror.

We sit in the living room and have a cup of tea. I tell her about Graeme and his kill realization.

'There's *Kil*imanjaro too,' she says. Then she says, 'I worry about Graeme. Do you think he's okay?'

'Of course he's okay,' I say. 'Why do you always have to feel sorry for people? As if your sympathy is going to help them.'

She says I could be a better friend to him, introduce him to people at school. If I cared I could do that, she says, but I don't care. All I think about's myself.

'Feeling sorry for someone diminishes them,' I say.

Mum says she can't believe she's raised someone so unkind, so unfeeling, so selfish. She's ashamed, she says.

I storm into my room, boiling with rage. From the kitchen I hear her sing 'Maggie May'. It didn't take her long to get over her worry. I think about Graeme a lot. I think about how unfortunate he is, and how I always try to avoid unfortunate people, too scared I'll have to accept their sadness, take on their loneliness. And Graeme is the most alone person I've ever met. It seems to gather round him, a testimony to the fact that he's different, that he's not like me or anyone else and never will be. It's not the same as other people's loneliness, loneliness that is bearable because it's rooted in the fluctuations of circumstance or time. Graeme's loneliness marks him out, and I don't want to be a witness to it. I don't want to be around it.

On Saturday afternoon, on my way out to meet Brona and Ann Marie, I bump into him and his mum, Jean, coming out of the Co-op. Graeme's a distance behind her, pushing her tartan happy shopper.

'I don't know why he doesn't go home,' Jean says to me. 'He's no use to me. More a hindrance than a help.'

Jean always speaks about Graeme as if he's not there, even if he's standing next to her. She tells me she can't do anything with him.

'He eats me out of house and home,' she says.

'My mum says I'm the same,' I say. I try to catch Graeme's eye, but he doesn't look up.

Jean says at least I'm getting my qualifications. She nods towards Graeme and says, 'That lump's got nothing to show for himself.'

'Graeme's just been unlucky,' I say. 'I might be too.'

Jean says people make their own luck.

'That's what I say,' she says. 'I tell him,' she says, 'I tell him who's going to have him like this?'

'Lots of people would have Graeme,' I say, trailing off. I blush.

Jean says they'd better be getting on. 'Come on, you,' she says.

Graeme unbrakes the wheelie trolley and looks at me quickly. Jean rolls her eyes at me as she hurries him up, and I pretend not to see.

Brona and Ann Marie are waiting outside Woolworth's for me.

'Hello, little homo sapien,' says Brona.

Ann Marie scowls and says why can't she talk like a normal person. I don't know why Ann Marie's friends with us. She calls me Brona's shadow and is even more hostile towards Brona, although Brona doesn't seem to notice, and when she does she thinks it's funny.

'Right,' Ann Marie says, 'I'm going in. D'any of you want anything?'

'You'll get caught,' I say, and Ann Marie says she won't. She says I'm not her mum, so shut it.

'Well I'll have *Just Seventeen* and an Aero then,' I say.

Me and Brona lean against the railings and wait for her. We talk about Ann Marie's outfit, the lycra skirt that shows her pants if she bends down, her red-white blotched knees, the flap of stomach that bulges from her t-shirt. Ann Marie always dresses like this, and sometimes it's embarrassing walking with her. Men look and don't do anything to hide the fact they're looking. Ann Marie likes the wolf whistles. She smiles at us triumphantly and raises her eyebrows as if to say: *There. I am attractive.* My mum wouldn't let me go out like that, but Ann Marie's mum does. Ann Marie says that if her mum tried to stop her, she'd change, but her mum doesn't try to stop her so she doesn't change.

Ann Marie comes out of Woolworth's with our stuff. She collects Forever Friends stationery, but she's got most of it now so she chucks it in the bin beside Iceland. We get the bus into town and go round all the shops in Argyle Street. In Topshop Ann Marie nicks Brona a pair of tartan tights, and some Clearasil in Boots for me. Then we sit in McDonald's for a while. Brona complains about having to babysit her little brothers again tonight. She says she's never going to have children.

'Motherhood is so *base*,' she says.

Then, while I'm complaining about my mum, Ann Marie stands up and starts shouting at us. She says we're both so horrible about our mums. We both think we're better than everyone else, with our big words.

'I'm going home,' she says.

I'm quite glad Ann Marie's gone. It gives me and Brona a chance to really talk. Brona loathes small talk. She uses words like that a lot: *loathe, adore, passionate, abhor, detest, horrendous,* words I'd be embarrassed to utter. We walk along to Charing Cross, and stand on the bridge watching the cars hurtling along.

'You know that song I played you?' I say. 'That Jackson Browne one? *Say a little prayer for the pretender who started out so young and strong only to surrender to the legal tender*. That's what worries me, you know. Being part of the rat race, justifying my life by making money. I mean,' I say, 'look at all these people down here. They only care about going somewhere, they're not in it for the ride.'

'That Jackson Browne made me want to puke,' says Brona. 'Mushy,' she says.

'I know what you mean,' I say quickly. 'It's my mum's CD.'

The sky is brilliantine heartless blue, no clouds, sun hitting onto our faces, bulleting off the cars. If I jump, I'll fly. Below us is the maze of motorway and pavement, coherent and impossible.

'Let's hitch a ride home,' I say.

'No way, we'll get the bus.'

I tell her my feet are sore. Suddenly a wave of euphoria washes over me, knowing I'm going to do it, knowing Brona's too scared to.

'If you do it,' she says, 'I'll smash your face in.'

'Scaredy cat.'

She comes and stands on the corner, next to the Starbucks, with me. After a few minutes a car stops and Brona grabs me. She says I've got to phone her right away when I get home.

'Okely dokely,' I say. 'If I remember.'

I open the car door and a woman smiles at me and asks me where I'm going. I turn round and wave to Brona as we move away. The woman's quite old with ridiculous earrings with dogs on them. I can't concentrate on what she's saying, I'm so delighted with myself. I'm actually a very timorous person, afraid of almost everything life can throw up, seeing danger in its innocuous ephemera – traffic, fireworks, spiders, heights, drunks, football matches, parks, cats, maths quizzes. I'm proud to overcome myself. If there was a war I'd be a draft dodger, but if I had to fight I'd probably do something reckless and dangerous, and people would think I was brave.

'Why are you hitching a lift,' the woman says, 'if you're only going to Shawlands?'

'Oh, my feet were sore.'

She says didn't I have my bus fare, and I say yes. Then she stops the car and says, 'Out.' I walk to the next bus stop and see the 38 pass with Brona sitting in the back. So I hide, and wait for the next one.

When I get home, Mum's not in. I listen to the answerphone and see Brona's phoned three times. I smile, thinking about her sitting at home worried. The doorbell goes and I run to answer it, thinking it's Brona. It's Graeme. He says he was just wondering if I'd like to go out tonight. The light from the close travels back and forth over one side, his hands dangling at his sides.

'I can't tonight, Graeme,' I say. 'I've got to do my homework. Can you not ask someone else?'

'No, not really,' he says. He pauses for a moment, thinking. He speaks with great lulls before each word, as if he's already disclaimed responsibility for what he's about to say. 'There's a guy I know in Skye,' he says, 'but I think he's too far away.'

I say he'll meet people in time, and Graeme says yeah.

'It's something I'm working on,' he says. 'I think this table tennis club tonight is a start. Do you like table tennis?'

'Not really. I don't really have time for that kind of thing with my GCSEs and all that.'

'Because we could go together.'

I tell him again how much homework I've got, how tired I am, and Graeme nods. He says he'll come back later in case I've finished my work.

At school we've got to write obituaries for ourselves. I've laboured hours over mine, trying to think what to write. It has to be the right mix of expectation and humility, something not too grand and not too risible. At last I settle on a documentary maker who challenges prejudices. Brona's is about her aspirations to be a sybarite. No one knows what this is except me, since Brona told me the other week and made me write it in the back of the vocabulary jotters we keep. She also wants to be remembered as a rock musician whose songs are poetry. Ann Marie's obituary is just two lines long: *Ann Marie won the pools and lived in a house by the sea. She was able to look after her mum and help needy causes.*

At lunchtime Brona says it was meant to be about her goals in life.

'Mine was,' says Ann Marie.

'What, you'd like to be remembered for being lucky?'

Ann Marie says there's worse things to be remembered for. She says she'd rather be remembered for that than for being a fuckin' sybarite, or whatever the fuck it was. She turns to me and says, 'Do you know him?' pointing at Graeme.

'Sort of,' I say.

'Well get him to come over,' she says. 'He's by himself.'

I wave Graeme over and say not to blame me if we can't get rid of him. 'You asked for it,' I say.

Brona sits on the bench reading her Plath compendium, and Ann Marie and Graeme and me stand together, shuffling our feet. I start going on about a French lesson I've just had, and out the corner of my eye I see Graeme take a comb out of his pocket and begin to pull it through his hair. Ann Marie's looking at him funny too, and I'm embarrassed.

'No need to spruce yourself up for us,' she says, and she smiles a lovely smile at him. 'What about you?' she says. 'What teachers you got?'

Graeme whispers a ream of names and I have to crane my neck towards him to hear. He's still combing his hair, flattening it out each side with one hand. He shakes his head, and we all watch, mesmerized, the dandruff float to the ground.

Walking back to class with Ann Marie I say, 'I'm sorry about that,' and she says, 'What're you sorry for?'

'About Graeme,' I say.

Ann Marie says what am I talking about, he's fine. She says he's missing a screw, but he's fine. 'You should have invited him over before,' she says.

Me and Mum stand by the window, watching Jean take suitcase after suitcase out to a removal van parked outside. Then two men carry out the sofa.

'What are Graeme and Tony going to sit on?' I say.

'I know,' says Mum, 'there's not going to be much left.'

They make a funny family, Jean, Graeme and Tony. I imagine Jean had suffered Tony courting her in a kind of passionless, inevitable way. I imagine long silences and Jean's dismay and briskness, and Tony's damp-handed, gentle dithering. And then their marriage. And Graeme. An aggrieved, put-upon Jean. I've been in their house once, and it was strangely sterile. The kind of house you can't imagine people laughing in, or crying in, or mugs accidentally being broken in.

'Look, the armchairs now,' says Mum.

'They'll have to squat on the floor like garden gnomes.'

Mum goes into the kitchen and I watch Tony and Graeme come out, and Jean giving them a hug. They all look alike from above, like characters modelled from plasticine. Their arms touch each other clumsily, doubtfully.

Graeme leans against my doorway, the wood creaking as he shifts the weight from his shoulder.

'So, is that your mum gone for good?' I ask. 'Has she left your dad?'

Graeme looks puzzled. 'She's living in Cardonald,' he says.

I ask him why he didn't go with her, and Graeme says the house only has one bedroom. Anyway, he says, it's too quiet for him up there.

'Here I've got the video arcades,' he says. He bites his lip and I notice it's started to bleed. Graeme doesn't realize, and does it again.

'I'd like to try a nightclub one weekend,' he says. 'What about you?'

'I think I'm too young,' I say. 'I'd better be going, Graeme, Mum's got tea on the table.'

'Yeah, okay.'

But he keeps standing there. I have to close the door. Listen to him remain outside, rocking on the balls of his feet.

Over dinner Mum says she thinks Graeme fancies me. She says would it be so bad to go on a few dates with him, and I say yes, it would.

'I don't want to talk about this,' I say.

Graeme's rock music reverberates up through the ceiling and me, dreaming of other boys, dreaming of all sorts of things that will one day happen to me, and things that will happen to the world because of me.

Brona likes to go over to my house at lunchtime because she likes talking to my mum. Sometimes, when I'm making tea, Brona disappears and I find her in Mum's room sitting on the bed, telling Mum what she's going to be. She says Mum's great, and sticks up for her when I call her a nutter.

'Ann's neurotic, not psychotic,' she says.

She says Mum's a lot zanier than me, and this pains me to the point of tears.

When we don't go up to my house, Ann Marie makes us go to Mr Boni's, where Graeme's now working. I dread this even more. Since Graeme's left school I don't see him so much, and I don't want him thinking I'm coming in to talk to him and rejuvenate our friendship. As soon as we go in, Ann Marie starts shouting at him.

'Hey, Speedy, serve me first, I've only been waiting two weeks.'

Graeme moves along the counter, peaked cap falling off when he reaches for the sweet jars. All the school kids in the queue laugh.

'Any freebies today, Grae?' Ann Marie calls out. 'Brona'll give you a kiss.'

'Will I heck,' says Brona.

Graeme drops soor plooms one by one onto the scales while Ann Marie leans over the counter watching him.

'One more. One more ... One more – Enough, enough.'

'Look' – he starts off with a faint air of assertion, but then it's gone. It's as if he's lapsed and then remembered himself – 'you said three ounces.'

'I'm only joking you,' Ann Marie says.

Outside, Brona puts on a funny voice and says Ann Marie lurrves Graeme. She wants to have his babies and make his tea and live with him for ever and ever.

'What if I do?' says Ann Marie. She stares at Brona close up. 'What's wrong with that?'

'Nothing,' says Brona surprised.

'But I don't, anyway.'

'Okay.'

She looks at us both and says she's sick of us. 'You're not kind,' she says, and then she storms away.

'Well,' says Brona, 'thus spake Zarathustra.'

I watch Ann Marie's back, her pathetic near-nakedness. 'At least we don't look like whores in distress,' I say, and feel guilty as soon as I say it.

A whole sorrowful summer passes. Brona's away with her grandparents in Nice, and I don't know what Ann Marie's doing. I work in a coat-hanger factory and cry on the way there, and again on the way home. The boredom is relentless and I come home and eat till I go to bed. Mum says I'm turning into a right little fat nanny boxer, and I don't talk to her for days. She buys me slim-a-soups and weight-watcher meals. I go on diets where I eat nine apples a day, or cabbage soup, and then, feeling overwhelmingly deprived, I gobble three bags of crisps before bed. Mum believes in the nobility of work and won't let me quit, even though she's not had a job herself in years. She says she's done her time, and now it's mine. I can't get her to understand that fixing metal hooks onto plastic frames is not only utterly bereft of nobility, but threatens to annihilate my spirit and will to live.

'Gets you out in the real world,' she says, and returns to her paint daubing.

I sit with Mavis, doing hooks. Mavis is about fifty with a kind of tremulous, over-ripe face and big watery eyes and lips that make me think of abused wives, although she's not. She's got an alcoholic husband and says she keeps a frozen leg of lamb in the freezer to wallop him with when he comes in drunk. She says it's called aversion therapy, although it's not worked so far. Now he's averse to coming home and stays in the pub all night instead.

Somedays Mavis doesn't talk to me much and sighs ostenta-
tiously when I make a mistake. On other days she tells me her life
story. This begins with her asking me what I've done the night
before (nothing or watched telly) and goes on with her launching
into the heady days of her own youth. When she was my age, she
was out every night. She'd no time to eat or sleep, she was out
that much. Not that she cared about sleeping and eating when she
was my age, with all the fellas chasing after her, and her flitting
around with them all, leaving them all dangling after her. That's
what you did then, she says, when you were young. She grabs my
arm and says she was gorgeous back then.

'Gorgeous,' she says, 'you should've seen me.'

'You're still good looking now,' I say, feeling ridiculous.

'See them all,' she says and waves her arm over the factory
floor, 'they'll all tell you how thin they used to be, but they
weren't. I've worked here for twenty-six years,' she says, 'and
they were always fatties – Teresa Doherty, Nan, wee Bettie,
always been big as buses. *I* was thin,' she says. 'Legs like a
whippet and skinny arms. Lovely legs,' she says. 'Frank said so
when we first walked out together. Nicest pins he'd ever seen, he
said.'

'I'd love to have thin legs,' I say, and Mavis says you've either
got them or you don't. When you lose them, she says, you never
get them back.

'I'll bring you in a photo and you can see for yourself,' she
says, but she never does.

Some mornings though, and for reasons unfathomable to me,
I wake up in high spirits. I wake up high as a kite. I want
to document the way the sun twinkles off a certain rib of tree,
the way the ground feels beneath my feet or the colour of the
abandoned plush armchair on the pavement in front of the
factory. I feel strong and usable and young, and hold my head
high, thinking other people must be thinking of me this way too.
On these days I think, *If Graeme fancies me, then other boys
might as well one day, and if Ann Marie fancies Graeme then that*

means him fancying me is not completely worthless. I stop by Mr Boni's and chap on the window. Graeme makes figures of eight as he wipes the counter, and he looks up and smiles. The next morning there's a bag of stale donuts, remnants from Mr Boni's, left on our doorstep.

In August we go back to school and find out Ann Marie's left. Brona says she'll miss her shoplifting. Over the summer Brona's got herself a French boyfriend who she did it with. In English she brings in letters he writes her, full of spelling mistakes and sentences like *I very much missing you*, which could be stilted English or a plaintive cry from the heart, I don't know. Brona says he's gloriously ugly in a Gerard Depardieu kind of way, although she decides to dump him one afternoon in Modern Studies. She says what's the point of having a boyfriend you can't have sex with.

'Actually,' she says, 'we didn't really have sex. I just sort of sat with him while he wanked off to porn mags.'

'Really?' I say. 'That's disgusting, why d'you do that?'

'I don't know, it was quite creepy. Do you know what else,' she says, and here she looks outraged, 'he didn't even know what a Nazi was. Can you believe that?'

'What an idiot,' I say.

'A total moron,' she says. 'He never washed his hair either, and it smelt really bad.' She leans back in her chair and says she could really be doing with a fag and a glass of red wine.

'What, you smoke now?'

'Sometimes,' she says. 'If I feel like it.'

'Could you teach me?' I say, and Brona says yeah.

'I think it looks really arty,' I say, and Brona says yeah, it does. She says we should go to the Stoat and Ferret tonight to try it out.

Me and Brona don't get into the Stoat and Ferret or the Wetherspoons. We manage to breeze up to the bar in Fix 2, but I get IDed and instead of trying to blag it I just walk out. Brona's mad at me. She says if I'd let her do the talking then we'd have got served.

'You look as young as me,' I say, and Brona says no, I look younger than her.

'No I don't,' I say.

'You do.'

'You're the one wearing demin shorts and tights,' I say.

We walk along Pollokshaws Road in silence. I suggest we try the off-licence, but Brona doesn't want to.

'The moment's passed,' she says.

'We could do the smoking thing,' I say, and Brona says she can't be bothered with that any more. I try to revive our earlier conversation about chess being a metaphor for life, but that doesn't work either. Brona says she needs to find some older friends.

'Thanks a lot,' I say.

'Once I knew them,' she says, 'I'd introduce you and then we could all go out together. Anyway,' she says, 'I'm offski.'

'Walk down the lane with me,' I say, and Brona says no, she's going the shortcut.

'Ciao for now,' she says.

I go down the lane anyway, even though it's getting darker, the sky vacant, closing in around me. I get scared walking down the lane with its quietness and the distance sketched in different shades of dark. Rain starts falling with a slow, methodical lull, and it's just after this that I hear something snap behind me. A shape lumbers up, and I see it's Graeme.

'Graeme, you gave me such a fright,' I say, barely able to contain my anger. 'Why're you creeping up behind me like that?'

'Sorry,' he says. He scrubs his forehead with his fist, and stumbles a bit.

I've not seen him for a while and am shocked by the way he looks. It's his teeth. They've gone all black, actually really black. When he speaks I see his tongue roll, furred and yellowed, and his breath's so bad I find it hard not to pull back. There's a repulsive air of decay around him which I want, instinctively, to move away from, to disengage myself from. His jeans are falling to expose a roll of white stomach, dirty pants-elastic. He looks straight at me in a glassy way that frightens me, and I start to hurry. I ask him what he's doing here anyway.

'It's not one of your usual routes home, is it?' I say.

'I'm trying to escape,' he says.

'From who, Graeme?'

'These people want to get me,' he says. 'They want to break my arms.'

I ask him why and he says he doesn't know. He shrugs, and I see he's shaking.

'I've got to run if they come,' he says.

'Well that's what God gave us legs for,' I say. 'Come on, we'll speed up.'

Everyone's been talking about the party for weeks. Me and Brona haven't been invited, but Brona says we should go anyway. The rumours are that Ann Brown's boyfriend is going to turn up and do something awful because she dumped him, and that Craig Ferguson is coming with magic mushrooms he grows in Pollok Park, and that Viki Green is going to wear a dress held together with safety pins. Brona says she wouldn't miss it for the world, she says we'll turn up and dazzle them.

'You know Clair Strang and that lot are going to the hairdresser's to get their hair done for it,' she says.

I roll my eyes. 'What are you wearing?' I say.

'You know that green dress in the window of Mum's shop?' she says. 'The one that makes me look like the Lady of Shallott.'

'Oh right,' I say. 'That's nice.' (Although actually it looks silly, peaked up at the front where a set of middle-aged bosoms should be.)

'Come round for me at seven,' she says.

'Right then, seven o'clock,' I say, and Brona says, 'Ciao for now,' and throws her hair behind one shoulder and strides away.

I feel tight-chested and sick as I walk home. Tim Lamont is going to be there tonight and in the past few weeks I think I've fallen in love with him. I've only spoken to him a few times, once in art class when he said he liked how I'd drawn a boot, and another time when he was sitting on the wall outside Burger King.

'What're you reading?' I'd said, and he'd said it was a Herman Hesse.

'Oh,' I'd said. I was upset that I hadn't heard of him and couldn't say anything. He sniffed and wiped his nose. He's always sniffing, always wiping his nose on his lumber shirt or a crumbled bit of kitchen roll. If he stopped sniffing and wiping his nose, I probably wouldn't love him.

'What does he write about?' I'd said, and Tim said he didn't really know.

'Kind of like, finding yourself and stuff,' he said.

I said I might read him then. 'Why are you sitting here anyway?' I said. 'Are you waiting for someone?'

'No, I'm just chilling. I felt kind of depressed today so I thought I'd better get out.'

'What're you depressed about?'

'Just life, you know.'

He's the only boy I know who's started to grow facial hair. It's pale and fuzzy, his entire face almost without colour, which gives him a look of constant, flummoxed, over-exposure. Sometimes he narrows his eyes and looks helplessly, unfocusedly lascivious, and I quite like that. Brona says there's something bovine about him, that he looks like a farmyard animal that's just been given a shot from a stun gun. She does impressions of him in a dopey, earnest voice saying *Um . . . cool like . . . kind of like . . .* and I laugh, and say nothing.

Mum tries to foist off some of her hideous clothes on me, her fruity-coloured patchwork skirts and baggy embroidered tops. She says I wouldn't know fashion if it pinged me on the nose. I decide on my black skirt and a black crocheted jumper I've got that manages to elude clinging to my stomach. I stare into the mirror, looking more and more unsatisfactory, more and more unlovable. Mum takes a picture of me sulking into the camera. She says she'll wait up to hear the gossip.

I walk round to Brona's house where her mum insists on painting our nails before we go. She says viper red would look startling with my black ensemble.

'I always say, girls,' she says, 'look after your peripherals and your peripherals look after you.'

'You say a load of rubbish,' says Brona, rolling her eyes at me with disdain. Brona's mum looks nothing like Brona. She's big and blowsy, with hulkish hands and legs that look like they could do a lot of damage. There are Virgin Marys and Jesus tea-towels and pictures of consumptive-looking saints everywhere. Once Brona bought a t-shirt with *Jesus is an Asshole* on it, and her mum tore it up with her bare hands and then cut it into a million pieces. Brona loved that.

'I think you've been reducing,' Brona's mum says, wagging her finger at me.

'Sorry?' I say, and Brona says, 'Dieting. She means dieting.'

I tell her I've been trying to eat healthily and Brona's mum says she has too. She says she lost a pound last week, and Brona cuts in and says she could have gone to the toilet, done a dump, and lost a pound.

'What a horrible daughter I have,' she says to me. 'Isn't she horrible? Now Veronica,' she says, 'would you like me to do your make-up? I used to work in cosmetics,' she says. 'I could do you some shading.'

'I'm okay, thanks.'

'Come on,' she says, 'it'll look lovely.'

'Don't let her touch you,' says Brona.

But I end up on the edge of Brona's bed being slathered in frosty pinks and bright orange, clammy face emulsion. I have to bite my lip to stop myself crying when I look in the mirror.

'Do you see how I've slimmed your cheeks down?' she says, pointing at the burgundy Cruella de Ville streaks down my face.

'It's lovely,' I say. 'Thanks.'

Outside I make Brona run to the public toilets at Queen's Park with me. She keeps stopping, bending over in laughter.

'You look like a clown,' she says.

'Fuck off.'

'Okay, I will then.'

'No, don't really,' I say. 'Come on, wait till I wash this off.'

Fiona's house is past the Newlands Safeway, into the near-suburban, near-city, maze of streets. I wait for Brona outside a shabby newsagent's that sells alcohol. Looking at the houses, the orangey lit-up windows here and there, I want nothing more than to be inside one of them, watching telly, and knowing that nothing bad will befall me while I'm there. No threatening, clamorous thoughts of Graeme or Brona or Tim. As we walk along, Brona's court shoes (borrowed from her mum) make an intrusive clank and I hear my own breath. She takes a swig of the Southern Comfort we've bought and says, 'A toast to soon getting the fuck out of Deadsville.'

'To the west, it's peaceful there,' I say, and take a swig.

I'm already drunk by the time we reach Fiona's. Brona links my arm with hers as we go up the garden steps. She says we're ready for the hoi polloi, but are the hoi polloi ready for us?

Fiona and some of her friends answer the door.

'Hello, little homo sapiens,' says Brona, and Fiona stares at her and says, 'Who invited you?'

'Heard it through the grapevine,' says Brona, and wafts past, with me following her. Tim is the first person I see when we go through the hall. He's slumped against the wall, looking like a well-fed street urchin and trying to smoke a cigarette that's gone out. The sitting room's been cleared except for a Welsh dresser which has fallen face down on the floor, surrounded by broken plates and china cups and crystal glasses. Fiona's now crouched over it, crying and saying her mum's going to murder her, but no one's taking much notice. We step over her to where all the girls are sitting.

'Well, here I am, people,' says Brona, wheeking off her velvet cloak.

'So you are,' says Clair Strang. 'How nice.'

Brona goes into the kitchen to get cups for our Southern Comfort, and I crouch uncomfortably on the floor, wondering if I look fat. Brona's a while coming back and I'm suspicious she's tanning down more than her fair share of our Southern Comfort. She wafts back into the room again and stands over us. She says we look like a miserable bunch of berries waiting to be plucked. If the boys are meant to be doing the plucking, they don't look too keen to start, huddled on the other side of the room, looking at the CD collection.

'It's been mental here,' says Viki Green, gravely. 'Sharon whited in the toilet and we had to call an ambulance.'

'Oh no,' I say, 'what happened?'

'Nothing,' says Viki, 'she's over there,' and she points to Sharon who's sitting morosely on a chair. 'The police came though,' she says, 'and took down her name and address and everything. When she told them she lived in Woodstock Avenue they laughed and said she was made for the weed.'

'You'd think they had something better to do,' says Lynne, 'than taking the piss out of poor Sharon.'

'No,' says Viki, 'it's serious, she could go down for this. We're all implicated,' she says.

I drink two paper cups half full of Southern Comfort. I watch Ann Quinn and Tony DiMaggio kissing in the alcove, becoming engrossed in the progress his hand is making up her skirt, the tiny, incremental moves. I become so engrossed I forget I'm staring at them until Ann's voice suddenly rings out with 'What're you gawping at?' and I turn away, blushing. The Prodigy, *I'm a Twisted Fire Starter*, is on full blast and throbs through my ears. I decide it's time to make my move on Tim. It's now or never. I slug my Southern Comfort and stumble into the hall.

'Hey there,' I say, and slump beside him on the floor beside the wall. The whole thing, I'm thinking, has to be executed with brazen comfortableness. The brazenness is feisty and risky but possibly rewarding; the casual easy-osy a back-up for rejection.

'Hey,' he says.

'I had to get out of that noise,' I say, 'it was doing my head in.'

He smiles at me but doesn't say anything, so I wait and don't say anything either. Brian Collins comes out of the bathroom and shouts, 'Hey, Tim, man,' and Tim salutes him by holding up his can of Carlsberg.

'Can I have a drink of that?' I say, and Tim says sure. I take a few gulps of it and hand it back. I ask him why he's not joining in the festivities and he says he just doesn't feel like it.

'Are you depressed again?' I say sympathetically, and Tim says yeah, sort of. He says he doesn't know what he's going to do with his life.

'Like today,' he says, 'I was in Waterstone's and I was going to steal a book. I actually had it in my pocket and everything.'

'What was the book?'

'Rilke's *Letters to a Young Poet*,' he says.

'Oh,' I say, 'I've not heard of that.'

'But man,' he says, 'I could've got caught and everything.'

'That'd be unlucky,' I say, 'to go to prison for stealing a book called *Letters to a Young Poet*. You wouldn't want the other criminals to find that out.'

Tim says yeah, but I can see his heart isn't in it.

'You could always lie if they asked you,' I say. 'You could always say it was called *How to Kill a Fucker*.'

'Right,' says Tim. Then he says, 'Who asking me what?'

'Nothing, it doesn't matter.'

I take another gulp of his Carlsberg. I look straight at him and say that I feel, in some way, that I've a connection to him.

'Do you want me?' I say. 'Just tell me yes or no.'

'Wow,' says Tim. 'This is heavy. I didn't know you felt that way. Wait here,' he says, 'and I'll go get another drink.'

I wait long enough, slumped against the wall, to realize he's not coming back. *Just go back in*, I tell myself. *Be easy-osy.*

*

In the sitting room, Brona's holding the floor, talking about how much she hates born-again Christians. I hear her say, 'All ministers are paedophiles.' I'm lying right over the couch, my arms and legs and face anaesthetized, heavy as cold fish. Their weight's too much for me, so I keep lying and don't care. The words, *Do you want me?* ring through my head, sounding more and more pathetic. 'I wouldn't want me either,' I say out loud (but quietly) and feel utterly dejected and sorry for myself.

At last someone stops the Twisted Fire Starter, and puts on *Revolver*. There's vague boy-girl dancing going on. Viki's got her face buried in Brian's jumper as if she's Scarlett O'Hara, and he's pulling faces behind her to his pals. Sharon and some boy I don't know are jigging about next to each other with impassive, strained faces, and some of the boys are jumping on each other's backs with emphatic heterosexual high-jinkery. Brona sits beside me on the couch, stroking my hair. She asks me what's wrong and just as I'm about to tell her I see Tim coming over. I heave myself off the couch, into a sitting position, wiping my hands in case we're going to have to hold hands and mine are all sweaty. The next thing I know Brona's jumped up from the couch and is standing beside him.

'Want to dance?' she says.

'Yeah, whatever,' Tim says.

Brona leads him right into the centre of the floor and begins snaking her hands up and down her body like she's stroking a fur coat. Viki comes and sits down next to me.

'Look at Brona,' she says, 'she's making a right arse of herself.'

I go through to the kitchen, but there's a bunch of boys I don't know sitting there, burning hash into yoghurts. One of them's asleep, his head on his arms. I sit in the toilet for a long time, dreading going out again. I dab my cheeks with cold water and avoid looking in the mirror.

When I go back into the room, I notice loads of people have left. I go over to where Tim and Brona are standing and as I get nearer Brona calls, 'What d'you think of Larkin, Ronnie?'

'He's okay,' I say. Neither of them looks at me. 'He had big milk-bottle glasses,' I say. 'He looked like a child molester.'

Brona says she likes 'They fuck you up, your Mum and Dad', and that it's disgusting we're not allowed to study it for higher just because it has the word fuck in it. She turns to me again and says, 'Tim here thinks he's outrageous.' She turns back to him and raises her eyebrows and smiles coquettishly.

'He's like, really misanthropic,' says Tim.

Brona says, 'What's wrong with that? That's a perfectly reasonable stance if you ask me,' she says.

'Well, no one asked you, Brona,' I say. 'I'm going home, I don't want to cramp your style.'

I'm sick on the pavement outside. A girl behind me asks if I'm okay and I nod without looking up.

'Well, take care of yourself,' she says.

I've no one to take care of me, I think. No one in the whole world. I hear the words, *Do you want me?* and weep afresh. Tim doesn't know what depression is. This is depression.

As I'm fumbling to open the close door, Graeme's dad comes up the steps.

'Well, that's Graeme getting treatment,' he says right away, with no preamble.

'Oh . . . That must be a relief to you,' I say, although I didn't know Graeme was getting treatment. The last time I saw him was in the lane a few weeks ago. 'Where's he at?' I say.

We go into the close together, stopping at Tony's door.

'Leverndale,' he says. 'It's for the best.'

He starts crying noiselessly, and I don't know what to do. Then he starts apologizing for the smell of his fish supper, and I say no, it smells nice.

'It's making me hungry,' I say weakly.

'He was thinking voices were talking to him, you know. Some wacky stuff he was coming away with.' He has his eyes down, and I want to say something, but don't know what. After a few minutes I say, 'I could send a get-well card.'

'Aye,' he says. 'Crazy stuff he was saying. Crazy.'

Their cat's pushing against his leg, mewing with a bored, white yawn, and Tony pushes it gently with his foot.

'I'd better be feeding this bugger,' he says.

Mum says she's surprised to see me back so early. It's only half eleven. She says she can smell the drink on me from here, and I let her rabble on.

'Graeme's in hospital,' I say suddenly.

'Oh no,' says Mum. She puts her hands to her face, covering her eyes, and says that sometimes you just don't want to know what's happening in the world. She says she knows it's been on my mind too, that we've all been worried about Graeme.

'You know,' she says, 'Sartre said that hell is other people, but it's not, is it? Hell is yourself.'

I don't know why I'm so angry at her, but suddenly I am. I tell her I'm going to bed, and Mum says at least tell her about the party. 'Come and sit down,' she says. 'Tell me everything.'

'No, I'm tired. Get your own life,' I say. 'Good night.'

Brona told me that after the party Tim walked her home. When she kissed him she bit his lip deliberately and it started bleeding, and Tim pushed her away because he said it was really sore. Now he goes in the opposite direction if he sees us. Brona says she was trying to re-enact Sylvia and Ted's first meeting, when Sylvia bit Ted's cheek at a party.

'But Tim is no Ted Hughes,' she says, 'to my Sylvia.'

'I thought Ted Hughes was a bastard,' I say. 'I thought he killed Sylvia.'

'He did. But still . . .'

Brona's got another boyfriend now, who she met outside the Spar. Every Friday night we meet him and his friends outside Central Station and one of them drives us places in his car. On the way there we drink everything they've bought and when it gets dark we stop and stand in a park or an industrial estate or somewhere, and the boys get their air rifles out and compete to see who can hit the furthest-away target. They all fancy Brona except for Mark, who has a little stub of ponytail and can do difficult sums really quickly in his head. He likes to take me aside and make me test him on his maths. He's got plans to be an accountant, not like the rest of them, he says, who only care about air rifles and Mad Dog. Apart from thinking that Kylie winked especially at him during her concert, he is wholly unobjectionable and not unhandsome. Brona says I should go for it. She says if it doesn't work out he might have friends I could get to know as a back-up position.

I'm on the bus, on my way into town to meet them. It's September, dark already. Outside the window the sky's old-tin colour, and it's starting to rain. I try to talk myself into fancying Mark, but I can't do it. Sometimes I can, and sometimes I can't. Even Mum's got a boyfriend now. He's a half-hearted biker with long hair, and he comes round to the house every third night. He brings round his *Young Ones* videos and sits laughing his head off at them. He's not a very deep person, and has a big, complacent gut, and I can't imagine what Mum sees in him.

We stop at Shawlands Cross and I see Ann Marie get on. It's been about a year since I've seen her, but she's not changed. I wave her over and she sits down beside me.

'Long time no see,' I say, and Ann Marie says, 'Yeah, have you missed me?'

'Yeah,' I say. 'Yeah. Have you missed us?'

'No.'

'Well, don't beat around the bush, Ann Marie.'

She says she didn't mind me, but Brona really got on her nerves.

'She just wanted to make me feel stupid,' she says, 'with all those big words she used.'

'That's just Brona's way,' I say.

'She acts like she's swallowed a dictionary,' says Ann Marie. 'She thinks she's cleverer than the rest of us.'

She leans back on the seat and lights a cigarette. We sit in silence for a few minutes, listening to Ann Marie's aggressive puffing. She tells me she's working in a hairdresser's, going to college twice a week for training. She says it's not all about being handy with a pair of scissors. There's biology of hair you've got to learn, she says, and all the different treatments, and what suits who. It's not just for dodos, she says. I ask her if she sees anyone from school, and she says no, she's glad to be away.

'That boy,' I say, 'who worked in Mr Boni's, he's in hospital now.'

'I know,' she says.

'How do you know?'

'I go up and visit him sometimes.'

'You go and visit Graeme?'

'Yeah,' she says, 'that's where I'm going now.'

The shock of Ann Marie visiting Graeme winds me, and I can't think of any appropriate response.

'How is he?' I say at last, and Ann Marie says fine, up and down.

'What d'you talk about?'

'Just whatever,' she says. She takes another long drag and stares out the window. 'I just tell him about what I'm doing,' she says, 'the girls in The Cutting House, anything.'

I tell her the last time I saw Graeme he was in a bad way. He was thinking people were out to get him, and Ann Marie says he's getting over that now.

'You just have to ignore it,' she says. 'Sometimes,' she says, 'you've just got to laugh.'

'Do you think he'll ever get better?'

Ann Marie shrugs and stares out the window again. She stubs her cigarette out on the window ledge and gets up.

'I need to change buses here,' she says.

Aunt Dorothy

'I am peripatetic,' said Aunt Dorothy. 'That means I travel around.'

I'm not sure Aunt Dorothy actually said this, but it sounds like something she might have said. When I think of her, I think of her sitting on a hard-backed chair, making a pronouncement. Her pronouncements are stately and grave; she does not talk the way anyone else I have ever met talks. She should be wearing a high-necked dress, and have a pinched, pointy face that darkens at times. She should look avenging. But Aunt Dorothy looked nothing like that. She was built like a rectangle and seemed larger than other people. Her face had a rough, uncontextualized look, the eyes and lips and nose too far away from one another, isolated-looking. She wore make-up but that always surprised me. She seemed the type of woman who would scorn such frippery-jippery.

Aunt Dorothy was my dad's big sister, eleven years older than him. He'd died when I was one and a half, in a fire at the garage he owned. Mum didn't talk about him much. The only thing she told me was that he was a right laugh. Her eyes would go a bit misty, as if she were remembering a sad film, and then she'd clap her hands and say there was no point, though, going over the past.

'The past is the past is the past,' she'd say, and squeeze my nose. To Mum, thinking about the past was, like alcohol and water-skiing and politics, pointless and unsalutary, and she could never understand why other people indulged in it.

When Aunt Dorothy came to visit, she would go down to the graveyard herself to see Dad. Mum hadn't gone since he died.

She said graveyards were morbid. (She didn't like hospitals because they were full of ill people, or big books because they were full of words, and she didn't like graveyards because they were full of dead people.) Once, when I was about ten, Aunt Dorothy took me. The graveyard wasn't gloomy and misty and dark, as I'd expected. It was like a huge park with lots of green grass shivering in the wind, and benches, and flowers, and people strolling. Aunt Dorothy marched along the tombstones, with me following. Every time she stopped I thought we were at Dad's grave, but it was only because something had tickled her fancy.

'Look,' she said, '*Mrs A Burns: Wife, Mother, and Daughter.* What do we think of that?' she said, and I said I didn't know, it was a shame she was dead.

'Is that how you'd like to be remembered? A Mrs Someone?'

'No, Aunt Dorothy.'

'Good,' she said.

It was a bit of an anti-climax when we got there. The gravestone looked like all the others, a grey-flecked marble block with gold lettering, faded in patches. I tried to think myself into the immensity of what I was witnessing, but couldn't. There was grass growing up the side, and a little plastic vase, but with no flowers in it. I stood looking at it, and past it, at all the other rows of stones, on and on and on. I never realized so many people had died. Aunt Dorothy was very quiet. In the gentlest voice I had I said, 'Did you and Dad used to have a right laugh?'

'We got on very well,' said Aunt Dorothy. 'Uncommonly well. There will never be anyone like him ever again.'

She tucked her scarf into her collar. After a few minutes she said that what was important was what wasn't written on the stone.

'See,' she said, '1952–1983. It's what's between the dash that matters. 1952–1983 doesn't tell you that when your father was your age he stuck a split pea up his nose and I had to take him to the hospital, and he laughed all the way. Or that he once got lost in the fog and when I went looking for him I found him on a street corner, calling my name. My history too,' said Aunt Dorothy, 'is between that dash.'

'I'd be really scared if I got lost in the fog,' I said, and Aunt Dorothy said so was Dad. He had a nervous disposition and was happiest just sitting with her, playing his Jew's harp.

'It's a pity he's not here to teach me how to play,' I said.

We stood and looked at the stone. After what I hoped was a respectful silence I asked her if Dad loved Mum, and Aunt Dorothy said she'd never got to the bottom of that one.

'Mum says all husbands and wives love each other,' I said, feeling a bit disconcerted.

We walked for another hour, till my legs were sore. Aunt Dorothy said to give her my digits, and held out her hand to me. I was embarrassed because I was too old to be holding adults' hands. Aunt Dorothy said it was because there were a lot of dogs around and they'd maul us soon as look at us. She asked me if I knew a good name for a large vicious dog, and I guessed an Alsatian.

'No, a mastiff,' Aunt Dorothy said.

She said that was a good word to describe thickset, powerful and vicious dogs, and she made me make up a sentence with mastiff in it.

I'm glad we've not seen any mastiffs today, but there's still time.

Aunt Dorothy laughed, and I felt pleased with myself. I was vaguely aware that it encapsulated the kind of sentiment she appreciated.

I think it was that day, too, that she quoted the Wordsworth poem: *I wandered lonely as a cloud, That floats on high o'er vales and hills, When all at once I saw a crowd, A host of golden daffodils.* I think we must have seen daffodils that day, but I don't know. I only remember the words, and how it struck me for the first time that words had power and possibility, that they contained the potential to personalize everything you saw or felt. Aunt Dorothy said Wordsworth plundered his ideas from his sister, her namesake, who wrote journals of everything they saw together. When she and my dad were younger, it was Dad who was the creative one. Aunt Dorothy said he knitted her a face cloth in Home Economics that she still has.

Aunt Dorothy was disposed towards illnesses of the unusual kind. Her own illnesses, and illnesses in general, were a kind of hobby, and she approached her subject with zealous frankness and enthusiasm. She was interested only in diagnosis, in spotting the possible onset of difficult and protracted, or brutally sharp and sudden, diseases. She catalogued them the way train-spotters note trains, with no interest in the wondrous finery and efficiency of their engines or knowledge of how to fix them.

'I'm dying here,' she'd say, coming up our stairs out of breath. 'My kidneys have been hurting all day.'

'Have you been to the doctor, Dorothy?' Mum would say, and Aunt Dorothy would say what was the point. They couldn't tell her anything she couldn't find out by looking up her medical dictionary. Aunt Dorothy had no respect for professional people, doctors or lawyers or dentists. She suspected they were out to gyp her. This always shocked Mum – *But they've got degrees and everything, Dorothy* – who'd only go to the doctor if her arm was hanging off, or to the dentist if a tooth was growing out of her cheek, and even then she'd be distraught at bothering them.

Often, during her visits, Aunt Dorothy would send me to her suitcase to fetch her medical dictionary. She'd pore over it, expertly flicking the pages as if she were reading a washing-machine manual.

'Ruth,' she called over once, 'let me see your hands.'

I held them up to her and she took each one by the wrist and held them in the air, side by side.

'That's okay,' she said, 'they're the same size. I just read there about a strange debilitating disease that children can get and one of the warning signs is that your hands are slightly different in size, and spade-like in shape. Of course,' she said, 'nobody tells you about it.'

'Quite right too,' said Mum. 'There's no point scaring folk.'

Aunt Dorothy knew many terrible tales. They usually involved people she knew or had heard of, and as I got older I began to think she made them up. She'd stare into space as if she was re-creating the scene of the tragedy right in front of her eyes.

'There was a girl I knew at school,' she'd begin. 'She was a nice girl, but full of foolishness. She tried too hard to get people to like her, and for that reason they never did.'

'What a shame,' said Mum.

Aunt Dorothy ignored any interruptions when she was telling a story. Mum never understood this. Talking for Aunt Dorothy was not a shared enterprise.

'This girl was the first one of us to get a boyfriend. Harold Chipwell – quite a dapper chap, worked in his dad's grocery shop. He tried to court me first, but I wouldn't have any of it. He wore a pinkie ring,' Aunt Dorothy said, as if this summed him up. 'Of course,' she said, 'I was very attractive then and had many admirers. Well this poor Edith at my school married him – she became terribly dowdy and downtrodden, stuck behind that grocery counter, and he didn't want children. Everyone said she wanted children but he didn't, and they said she'd do anything for him. But a few years later he left her. Left her for someone else and had three children by her. They're very happy, by all accounts.'

'That was her had it then,' said Mum. 'That was her had it: no man and no children. Poor Edith.'

'Yes,' said Aunt Dorothy. 'And she still works at a grocery store.'

I said maybe she met someone else. Maybe she adopted. Or maybe she decided she didn't want to be tied down anyway.

'No,' said Aunt Dorothy. 'I saw her in the town a few months back, working in the Spar. She looked unhappy and desperate to tell someone off.'

I tried to create alternative stories for Edith. When she got home from the grocery store, she fell into the arms of her lover; she went to Salsa classes and singles bars and drank vodka and tonics; she nursed exquisite pain; she wrote beautiful love poems in a big diary at night. But I couldn't do it. I could only see Aunt Dorothy's version – the silly girl who used to put lemon juice and curlers in her hair to look like Doris Day, but now had a face like a tobacco pouch. Someone once giggly and carefree who'd fallen for a rake with a pinkie ring. He'd left her without a backward glance, and now she was all alone and bitter, presiding over dusty tins of peas and pints of milk. I couldn't triumph over Aunt Dorothy's version of events, and neither could anyone else. Collectively her stories were a body of evidence: *See, yet another poor bastard!*

'Imagine someone doing that to you,' said Mum. 'Wasting your whole life like that.'

'Yes,' said Aunt Dorothy.

There was a kind of relish in the way her stories always ended with Aunt Dorothy sealing her character's fate. No glimmer of hope left, something snapping shut.

All Aunt Dorothy's stories were bleak, even the funny ones. A man on TV who'd had his hand cut off by the bread-slicer in the Mother's Pride factory. He'd been the first patient ever to try a new transplant surgery, a dead man's hand sewn on to his stump. The hand began to decay, and he started to realize that people were shaking him by the wrist.

'The upshot of it all,' said Aunt Dorothy, 'was that he had to have it lopped off again.'

'That's a sin,' said Mum. 'Having to get your hand off twice like that.'

Later, I told my friends about Aunt Dorothy and her stories, her exact, school-mistress way of speaking, as if she'd learnt English in Victorian times. I laughed imagining her going on her pilgrimages to visit her heroes' old haunts, their houses and places of work. Those huge, quivering knees of hers carrying her up hills and across cities to catch a glimpse of a street that Dickens mentioned in *Little Dorrit* or Boswell's house. She had whole galleries of heroes and heroines, usually writers whose names I strain to remember, but can't. She had a massive store of anecdotal knowledge about them that I enjoyed listening to. Once, sitting in an English lecture about Mary Shelley's *Frankenstein*, I suddenly recalled her telling me about Mary's epically tragic life. Her elopement at seventeen, her three dead children, her stepsister's suicide, the suicide of Shelley's wife, her famous feminist mother and anarchist father.

'And all in a few short years,' said Aunt Dorothy admiringly.

'So she ran off with someone else's husband?' said Mum. 'That's very nice. These women writers,' she said, 'they don't seem to play by normal people's rules. I mean, that Jackie Collins one, how many times is it she's been married now? Three, isn't it?'

Aunt Dorothy said she wouldn't know about that, and Mum said she'd heard her books were risqué. She hadn't read any herself. In fact, she said, the last book she'd read was at school, and here was me, her little bookworm.

'She takes after James,' said Aunt Dorothy. 'He was a great reader. And myself, of course.'

'Yes, she must do,' said Mum absently. She got up from her seat and clapped her hands. 'Do you know what I feel like?' she said. 'A big bowl of raspberry ripple ice-cream. Any takers? Dorothy,' she said, 'a big bowl of raspberry ripple for you?'

Aunt Dorothy told me how *Frankenstein* started off as a ghost story, how on holiday Byron and Shelley and Mary had a competition to see who could write the scariest story, and Mary's became *Frankenstein*. I remember how that same week, inspired, I wrote my own scary story and typed it up, presented it to Aunt Dorothy. I was immensely pleased with it. It was entitled *Perishing*: the first line was *It was a perishing night*, and the last line, *She saw the knife glint in the dark but before the scream left her lips she perished*. Aunt Dorothy said it was a very sophisticated piece of work, and that she was going to take it to her friends to show them what a talented niece she had.

'I am peripatetic,' said Aunt Dorothy. 'That means I travel around.'

I don't know who else she visited. Mum and I were her only family. She used to mention friends she'd just been to, or friends she was just going to, but she never said much about them. They were mostly women. She had money from her mother's will, half of which Dad had got, and a house somewhere in Cornwall. We'd never been invited down there. In her more disgruntled moments it was something Mum complained about.

'Well that's Dorothy back to Cornwall,' she'd say, 'if that *is* where she comes from. Fifteen years,' she'd say, 'and never so much as an invite.'

'But Aunt Dorothy travels around, Mum,' I'd say. 'Maybe she's never at home.' And Mum would say, 'I suppose so. Anyway,' she'd say, 'me and you're real homebirds. It'd be a trek down there.'

It crossed my mind when I was older that Aunt Dorothy may have been gay, but it wasn't an interesting line of enquiry. I thought her above, or beyond, relationships which involved sympathy and desire and compromise and messiness. The idea of her having sex with anyone was unimaginable.

Aunt Dorothy never phoned before she arrived. She might have been refused, or excuses could have been made. She would appear from nowhere, scrambling Mum's domestic routine, and then disappear again. Mum was always relieved when she went, and I guess the other people she visited must have been too. I always wondered if Aunt Dorothy thought about the impact she had on people, and if she did, what were her conclusions?

I would see her first, usually from the window, or when I was playing in the street or walking home from school, and I'd run and tell Mum.

'Dashhounds,' she'd say. 'Tell me you're joking. She's only just left.'

'Mum, don't be so anti-social,' I'd say.

She'd look around the room frantically, as if she was hoping to find a hiding place. 'Dashhounds to heavens,' she'd say.

I liked Aunt Dorothy coming over because it didn't unsettle my routine in any way, but meant staying up late and nice teas and Aunt Dorothy taking us places in her car. I would trail Mum down the hall as she opened the door.

'Oh Dorothy, lovely to see you.'

Aunt Dorothy would stand there, enormous as ever. She'd say she was just passing through and thought Mum might like some company.

'Funny you should say that, Dorothy, I've got my aerobics club tomorrow night.'

'That's nice for you,' said Aunt Dorothy.

She sat herself firmly and proprietorially on the sofa, and opened the big leather bag she brought everywhere with her.

'For you and for you,' she'd say.

Mum and I always got a present. Something we really wanted before we even knew we wanted it. Mum got hand-painted thimbles, which she collected, and sometimes hatpins, which she also collected, but wasn't as fond of. One Christmas she got a display cabinet for them, a little square wooden thing with glass partitions for each thimble to fit snugly inside. Mum loved that and put her brass animal collection inside it, but not her special thimbles, which remained, bizarrely, in an old shoebox in her room. (It always makes me laugh remembering her telling Dorothy how she loved things in miniature. *They're so cute, aren't they?* and Dorothy's big impassive face staring back at her.) I got a rubber stamp with red and green and gold ink. I got a snowstorm with the Empire State Building inside, a diary with a key and thick yellow pages I was afraid to write on, a thesaurus, a rhyming dictionary, a silver necklace with a dangling fairy trinket.

'You've got to stop doing this, Dorothy,' Mum would say. 'It's too much, it's far too much,' and she'd look sideways at her thimble with both longing and dismay.

'Thank you very much, Aunt Dorothy,' I'd say, itching to get into my room and try out my present.

'When I was a small girl,' she'd say, 'I enjoyed writing in my diaries and I still have them now.' Or, 'A little boy I once knew had a rhyming dictionary just like that one, and now he's a poet. Not a very good one, it has to be said.'

'Are you staying for tea, Dorothy?' Mum would say. (There was always the hope, on Mum's part, that Dorothy might have just popped over and would pop away again just as soon. It never happened.)

'Yes, if it's not any bother?'

When Aunt Dorothy asked a question she never seemed to expect a reply. It was merely as if she were dropping a statement into your lap.

'Of course it's no bother,' said Mum dejectedly.

One time, on a rare occasion when Dorothy had phoned in advance, Mum had prepared a special dinner. I was excited, telling her that Mum had made her special soup, and how gorgeous it was.

'I hope you've not gone to any palaver on my account,' Dorothy said, and Mum said no, it was no bother.

'All you need,' Mum said, 'is a tin of Heinz condensed tomato soup and a tin of Heinz condensed chicken soup. I just mix them together and then I grate in my own carrot.'

Aunt Dorothy said it sounded interesting. She said that if she was hungry enough she could eat anything.

'I see you've done up the kitchen,' she said.

'Yes,' said Mum, 'me and Ruthie did it ourselves.'

'Is that blancmange colour in fashion at the moment?' said Aunt Dorothy, and Mum said, 'Oh no, Dorothy. It's not blancmange. Petal Pink, it's called. Ruthie,' she called to me, 'go and get that tin of paint in the attic to show your Aunt Dorothy. Petal Pink it is, Dorothy. That's what it says on the tin.'

'If you say so. I call it blancmange.'

When Aunt Dorothy was staying there were certain things she liked to do. She liked to go on day trips, sometimes by herself, to places of historical interest, and she liked to talk about them afterwards. She liked nature programmes, although not ones about dogs or cats or insects – not ones about banal, innocuous animals. She said she only had to look around her to see commonplace creatures going about their commonplace business. She also liked to read in her room (which was my room with me displaced to the fold-down sofa in the sitting room). She brought a travel electric kettle which she took up to her room and made cups of tea with. Sometimes I went up and sat with her. I was always a bit nervous because she spoke to me seriously, as if I was on equal terms with her and would be judged on that basis. It was on one of those days she told me about her near-death experience. It happened in a friend's house in Colchester. Her heart stopped beating for a few minutes. She couldn't prove it to the doctors, but that's what happened. In those few minutes she saw the faces of all the people she knew flash before her, and she heard what they were thinking of her.

'I lost many friends after that,' she said, 'because during those few minutes I found out that many of them had wronged me in thought or deed.'

'Was I there?' I asked, and Aunt Dorothy said I was, but that I was rooting for her to live.

'I would have been,' I said seriously.

Aunt Dorothy said that since that time her powers of perception were heightened. Sometimes she even saw things that were going to happen in the future.

'So I could ask you something,' I said, 'and you could tell me if it was going to happen?'

'Well, perhaps.'

I couldn't think of anything to ask her, though, and sat thinking for a few minutes.

'Did Mary Queen of Scots scream when she got her head chopped off?' I said at last. Aunt Dorothy said she'd never looked into the past before. She said she'd have to think about it and write down her answer for me. A couple of hours later there was an envelope on my makeshift pillow. It was addressed to me in Aunt Dorothy's spindly copperplate writing. Inside it said: *No, Mary Queen of Scots did not scream when she got her head chopped off.* At the bottom of the page was: *Goodnight from your Aunt Dorothy X.*

When I left home I didn't see Aunt Dorothy for years and I never thought about her. I was living three hours' drive away from my mum, whom I missed, in a flat with no heating and rusty-coloured water. I loved my flat because it was all mine and I thought even the squalor was beautiful. It was the kind of squalor, I thought, that someone carefree and busy might accumulate, even though I was neither. Three afternoons a week I taught English students and in between I was meant to be working on my Camus thesis. All I'd decided on was my title. I stared at it typed out on the page for hours, trying to see past it, or round it, trying to calm myself. I never did any work on it, or if I did it was something I'd pilfered from a textbook and tore up the next day. I wanted to be out in the world, not sitting at home struggling to pretend I thought things I didn't. My main problem was that the bit of world I moved in offered me little in the way of social intercourse. Frankly, I felt let down. There was the newsagent's downstairs, the supermarket, and a few hours with my fellow tutors in the student tearoom after my Friday classes. I was jealous of their boyfriends, their confidence, the smooth, mindful quality of the lives I imagined them to lead. I even began to resent Camus. At least he had a good social life and was lucky with the ladies.

I felt I was capable of goodness, but there was no one there to vent my goodness on. I went through a phase of talking to *Big Issue* sellers, but one of them pick-pocketed my purse, and another one followed me down the road begging me to let him kip at my place.

So I became self-absorbed. Since there was no one there to stop me, I threw myself wholeheartedly into any neurosis that entered my head. At times I felt as if I was standing back and observing my life like an experiment. A project. I watched and waited to see how far I could go, and what the consequences would be. My most enduring fear was of physical violence. First it was punches. I was terrified of being punched as I walked down the street, terrified of witnessing someone else being punched. Then I graduated to being afraid of underground stations, railway stations, the edges of pavements, going down the stairs on buses. It would be so easy, I figured, for someone to come up from behind and push me. And it wouldn't just be me that would get hurt, or possibly die, but other people too. Both arbitrary and intentional violence spoke to me of equally chaotic and terrifying worlds in which retreat was the safest option. So I retreated to my flat, sometimes for days on end, only going downstairs to buy milk and cigarettes.

And while all this was happening, there was Rob. I'd met him busking outside Somerfield one day. It was on one of those days I'd decided to talk to someone, anyone, if it killed me. We went out every day for about three weeks and then it just tailed off. He stopped phoning me so much, the days between our dates got longer and longer. He played the cello in a street band and was away a lot travelling with them. I never knew when he was at home and when he was away, so I waited for him to phone and tell me to meet him. I felt capable, at times, of going to desperate and wild measures for him. Following him down the road; hauling him out of pubs; tear-soaked late-night letters and arguments. But I never did any of these things. This, at least, confirmed my obdurate sanity, no matter how I strove to lose it. I never knew him well, if at all, but I thought about him all the time. *You've just got to enjoy yourself,* he'd say. *I never worry about what other people think. Things sort themselves out. Why not have a good time now instead of worrying about tomorrow? I'm always content.* Outrageous things that I thought no one could possibly believe, until I met Rob. He liked to be amused, and was amused easily. He liked anecdotes – I saved up funny stories from the *Metro* newspaper to tell him.

'That's a beezer,' he'd say. He'd say, 'Tell me that one again about the pig's lug. The guy getting the pig's lug in his sandwich . . .'

He sent me a couple of letters, which surprised me. They were full of descriptions of his dreams, the mating habits of sperm whales, a slippery piece of music he'd mastered. They were never about what he'd seen or done or heard when he was away. Never about the humdrum passage of his days and hours. When I asked him about his parents or his friends he'd say he didn't know how to describe them. 'They just are,' he'd say. 'Anyway,' he'd say, 'I don't like talking about people when they're not here.'

'They're not going to care.'

'It doesn't matter, I still don't like it. Anyway,' he said, 'I've told you I'm pathologically uncurious about other people. You, on the other hand, are a nosy parker.' He yawned and said, 'As Hemingway wrote, talking's a load of guff. Have I told you how sexy you look today? Come over here, sexy . . .'

So I waited, and acted casual. Tried to be hapless and cute and entertaining. Once, leaving his flat and not knowing when I was going to see him next, I'd called, 'Remember, Jesus and I love you.' It was the only time I'd ever said it to him. I was embarrassed. I had to recapitulate, turn it into a joke. *Jesus and I love you but everyone else thinks you're an arsehole.*

'Ah, but they don't have the power of the mighty cello behind them,' said Rob.

I looked at him all the time. I looked at his face and knew that one day I would not remember it, and how terrible that knowledge was.

Then, one Saturday morning, I got a phone call from mum warning me that Aunt Dorothy was on her way over. She said she was sorry.

'Muggins here gave her your address,' she said. 'I thought it was so she could send you a birthday card.'

She said she knew I probably had plans for the weekend (I did: it was waiting for Rob to phone me) and that I should just pretend I wasn't in. Dorothy would never know.

I kept the curtains closed. Rain bounced off the windows, creating an intense, otherworldly silence around the rooms in my flat. I lay on my bed with the phone beside me, looking at the sky to mark time, looking at the drop of early winter darkness. I decided that if Rob phoned before three then I'd arrange to meet him and ignore the buzzer if Dorothy turned up. And then it was four o'clock, and I gave him an extra hour. I hated that phone. It lashed my heart how much I hated it, and hated myself for waiting on it, and hated Rob for not phoning. And then, when the buzzer finally went at quarter to five, I jumped up and lifted it like it'd been my intention all along.

'It's your Aunt Dorothy,' she said.

'Oh right, come up.'

She didn't look much older, although it was over five years since I'd seen her, still enormous and unavoidable and present. But as we went through the hall I realized how slowly and painfully she was walking, how she wasn't enormous any more, but smaller than me. She had a big wobbly stomach now, as if the fluid in her body had collected like a lifejacket round her middle. Maybe she had always looked like this, but it was a shock to me, then, to see how vulnerable she was.

'I was just visiting some friends in the area,' she said. 'Clair and Alan Black,' she said, 'you may know them.'

It made me smile hearing Dorothy again, suddenly remembering her special way of talking, as if she were doling out edifying little taps of a mallet.

'No,' I said, 'I don't know many people here.'

'They are very bored with each other,' she said, 'so they welcome my company.'

In the sitting room I put my arms in the air and laughed, welcomed her to my pad.

'It's a bit of a messaplantania,' I said.

Dorothy's gaze took in everything whole, like a gulp. 'Does the smell not bother you?' she said, and I said I was used to it.

The room smelt of smoke and old rubbish I hadn't taken out yet. It seemed suddenly dismal and hopeless, shadows big as whalebones streaking the walls. I offered to open the window, and Dorothy said I could if I wanted.

'I'm not bothering you, am I?' she said, and I said no, I was just going to watch telly.

'Addles the brain,' she said.

'What's that?'

'Television. I'll have no truck with it. Except for the wildlife programmes, I like those.'

I said I remembered that, from years ago, Dorothy's wildlife programmes. I discovered sloths weren't necessarily lazy watching one of those programmes with her.

'You've got a good memory,' she said, and I said I remembered lots from the times she came to stay.

'Really?' said Dorothy, and she smiled and made me wish I could say more, but I was embarrassed and didn't. I went through to the kitchen to put the kettle on, and she followed me through.

'Here,' she said. 'I almost forgot. This is for you,' and she put a wrapped box on the sideboard.

'Oh Dorothy, you shouldn't have bought me anything, you really shouldn't. I'm too old now for birthday presents,' I said, and Dorothy said I was still little to her.

Later on Dorothy went for a bath while I made spaghetti in the kitchen. I couldn't imagine her naked and alone in the bath, couldn't imagine her in her silent hours of repose and weakness. I realized that although I'd known her all my life, I knew nothing about her. I didn't know if she had ever worked, if she had had a lover, what her house was like. And I couldn't ask. It was understood Dorothy would not countenance that type of question. She was a fantastic adjudicator of conversation. She set the tone and subject of what was to be discussed; she made it clear that only the minimum response was required. I wondered if many of the people she visited resented this kind of bullying, her denial of any reality but her own. And Dorothy herself. Did she ever look back and realize that no one really knew her, no matter the beautiful presents, the visits, the days out? Did she resent no one trying to cajole her, to question, to find out?

When she appeared from her bath, fully dressed and with her hair dried, I decided that I was going to take control of the conversation. I was going to make her talk. So, while Dorothy was occupied eating, I asked her if she had ever wanted children.

'What a strange thing to ask,' she said, and instantly I was embarrassed and made up some excuse about her liking children.

'Well,' she said, 'I like some children, but by no means all of them. Some children nowadays are extremely ill-mannered.'

She was silent after that, and I put all my efforts into resisting the silence. After a bit she said, 'Well, see, it was different in my day. If you weren't married by the time you were twenty-three you were left on the shelf. You were a spinster. And although I had many suitors myself, I didn't want to be ironing and scrubbing and having tea on the table for any of them. That was not the kind of life that appealed to someone with my spirit. I always preferred talking to men and letting the other women do the ironing and washing and cooking.'

She took another robust fork-load of spaghetti and considered.

'At parties,' she said, 'I would always be talking to the men, and the women would be twittering away in the kitchen making sandwiches, and they'd come in and see me, and they'd rush over and start clutching at their husbands. It really made me laugh.'

'What did you do,' I said, 'when the women did that?'

'I just ignored them, of course,' said Dorothy, 'and kept on enjoying myself.'

I said the women might have had interesting things to say too, and Dorothy said those particular women didn't. 'Nor did the men either,' she said, 'it was just fun to see them all squirm. The wives were jealous of me,' she said finally, 'because I was free and they weren't.'

And so the moment passed, and I was still no closer to knowing if Dorothy had wanted children, or what she ever wanted. She had a peculiar and disorientating knack of turning every incident of her biography into an illustration – the exemplary heroine cast before your very eyes. And yet, there was bitterness. There was bitterness in what she said. It surprised me. I was free, she said, and the words seemed to reverberate after she'd spoken. It was the kind of freedom I was afraid of.

*

That night Dorothy slept in my bed, and I slept on the living-room couch, like the old days. We got up early the next day and went on a day-trip in her car. A jaunt, Dorothy called it. I can't remember where we were meant to be going. The car broke down temporarily and then we got lost. Periodically Dorothy berated the car directly – *Now this just isn't good enough. Pull your socks up* – something she used to do to make me laugh when I was little. I found this difficult to respond to now I was an adult. I don't know why, but it made me a little sad. We arrived at Balloch about three. The sky was charcoaly, darkened above the loch, the water ripped black and blue and violent. Wind sliced through my clothes, and pulled us back and forth like puppets. Dorothy lent me a green windbreaker she had in the car, a ridiculous thing that ballooned around me and tied below my knees. I thought about what Rob was doing, if he was trying to phone me, and not knowing made me feel panicked and depressed. In one of the gift shops Dorothy bought postcards, and then we went into the café next door. We sat by the huge plate-glass windows, drinking coffee. I thought we must have looked an odd couple – Dorothy with her interrogative, long stare, unsmiling, and me with the clownish jacket, exhausted and worried. We both looked displaced somehow. Dorothy said that contrary to what some people might think she was not a naturally gregarious person, and that she enjoyed just watching the water. It was nice, she said, just sitting here watching. Experiences were always better, she said, when someone was there with you.

The wind died down and we left the café. We walked past little rows of houses, a closed chip shop, and a hairdresser's with three women sitting talking inside. A tourist couple passed us with cameras dangling round their necks, and then a man walking his dog who said hello to us. The shore was stony, littered with grey blobs of jellyfish. We sat on a bench and looked out at the lights dimming and twinkling distantly across the loch. I said to Dorothy how strange it was being around so much sky. I wasn't used to being confronted with sky, I said, and Dorothy said it was living in Glasgow. In Glasgow you're deprived of sky. I said I knew it was a cliché, but the scenery here made you feel small, it made you feel other things were a million miles away and not important. I could almost get religious, I said, looking at this, and Dorothy said yes, it gave you certain intimations, no matter how you resisted them.

'I think I'd like to live somewhere like this,' I said. 'Somewhere small like this. You kind of feel life would be more manageable here. You'd know everyone.'

'Why ever would you want that?' said Dorothy. 'You're just young, you wouldn't want to be stuck somewhere like this. Anyway,' she said, 'they're all alcoholics here. It's the boredom.'

'But it's like . . .'

I looked out at the sky, how beautiful it was, and thought of the little rows of houses and the group of teenagers in the café, and the women in the hairdresser's. And all the noise of other things was silent, and I wanted to tell her everything and not care what I said. I just wanted to talk and to hear what Dorothy would say.

'It's like,' I started off, 'it's like in Glasgow everything's so big, it's so big and unmanageable, and I get into these routines of only going to the same places, the same pub, the same shop, the same bus, and I'm always hoping to see someone I recognize. Not even someone I know, but just a face that I recognize. But I hardly ever do, and sometimes I go home and I have this sense, I have this sense that something really careless is going on, that I can't even manage to place myself in the world as other people do. And I don't know, it might be the world's fault, or it might be mine. But somewhere small, like this, it'd be much easier. It'd be like your surroundings were already whittled away just enough to accommodate you. It'd be easier.'

'Life's never easy,' said Dorothy, 'no matter where you live.'

'I know, I know.'

I was embarrassed suddenly, hardly aware of what I'd just said, but only an impression of myself rambling, melodramatic.

'I'm sorry, Dorothy,' I said, 'I'm talking rubbish. I mean, I must sound so weak to you. You're always going new places, you're peripatetic.'

'Sometimes,' said Dorothy, 'people are only peripatetic when they've not found their own small place. Maybe they'd stop if they did. But anyway,' she said, 'you're young. You're not weak, you're just young. What you're feeling just now,' she said, 'it'll pass. I know it will.'

'I don't think it will,' I said, on a roll now. 'There's this boy I know, and he's part of the problem because I think about him a lot. I know he's around about the place, but I never see him. There's always the possibility of bumping into him, but I don't. He doesn't feel the same about me,' I said. 'In the nicest possible way, he doesn't care if he sees me or not. Have you ever really missed someone? Like someone you can't get out of your head?'

Once I stopped talking I was exhausted and light-headed. That was it. I'd told her everything, and it was all done, down on a platter.

'No,' said Dorothy, 'I don't think I ever have felt like that. I imagine I was much too interested in myself to be that interested in anyone else. Come on,' she said and put her hand lightly, just quickly, round my head. 'We'd better go before it gets any darker.'

That Tuesday I came home from teaching and found Dorothy in the living room, reading her book. I made us a cup of tea and out of nowhere she said she'd been considering what I asked her, about ever missing anyone, and she remembered there was someone. When she was a young woman, she said, she used to help her mother out in her dress shop, and there was a girl who worked there, Isobel, whom she became friends with. After work Dorothy would pull the blinds over the shop window and they would stay behind and talk for hours, just the two of them. But then, after some months of this, Isobel's mother turned up at the shop and said that Isobel wasn't to stay behind with Dorothy any more. It wasn't natural for them to be sitting so long into the night when Isobel was engaged and had her wedding to attend to.

'We were true friends, me and Isobel,' said Dorothy, 'but soon after that she stopped working in the shop altogether and when I sent her a birthday present – it was a beautiful gold bracelet,

Isobel had very slender wrists like yourself – well, she sent it back. I remember I was quite upset about that.'

'And what was she like?' I said. 'Isobel. What was she like?'

'Well, let me see. She was a very serious person, everyone thought she was too quiet, but she wasn't with me. We used to like to talk about the people who came into the shop, our impressions of them. We thought the same about things. I remember some of the customers complained about Isobel because they thought she was glaring at them. She wouldn't wear her glasses and had to scrunch up her face and squint to see things properly, so they complained about her glaring. And Isobel would approach them, very demurely, with her hands crossed, and explain to them that she was myopic. That was the word she used, *I'm afraid I'm myopic*, all sweetness and light and apology. And the funny thing,' said Dorothy, 'was that she probably was glaring at them. Isobel couldn't abide many of the customers. She hated small-mindedness and stupidity, like I do myself.'

'And did it take you long to get over Isobel?' I asked, hesitating since I wasn't quite sure what Dorothy was telling me. Also I was insatiably, ruthlessly curious about romances, especially broken ones, believing I might somehow work out probability rates for my recovery by studying other people's.

'Not that long,' said Dorothy. She picked up her book and started to read. This was one of her ways of terminating a conversation. No beating about the bush. 'A few years,' she said.

'A few years?' I said, dismayed. After a few minutes of silence I said, 'And did Isobel resent her mother for splitting you up?'

'That I shall never know,' said Dorothy.

Dorothy stayed for the rest of the week, but we never returned to the subject of that conversation. During the day I went up to the library to study and Dorothy pottered around museums and galleries. At night we had our tea together – twice she took me out to a restaurant – and then we read our books or watched telly. Dorothy was reading Boswell's diaries, a book which delighted her, and made her laugh out loud. Sometimes she would read me out a funny bit, Boswell striding around a room admiring his fabulous ruffle and dashing figure. She said he was quite a character and that she would finish the book and give it to me before she left. (That concerned me somewhat, since there seemed to be a fair whack still to be got through, and my back was aching from sleeping on the couch, and by night-time my ears rang with the sound of her voice). The television was more dubious territory. Once we started watching an innocent romantic comedy only to be confronted with an interminable huffing and puffing sex scene, my embarrassment only relieved when Dorothy said, 'Shall we turn this rubbish off?' We never watched telly again after that.

On the way home one day I bought her a dream catcher from a craft stall outside the library. I wrapped it up and wrote To Dotty on the front, but for some reason I was too embarrassed to give her a present. It seemed inappropriate for me to actually give Dorothy something, and something so sentimental and silly. I ended up unwrapping it and handing it to her in its paper bag with as little ceremony as possible.

On Friday night Dorothy announced her departure.

'Well that's another week wasted,' she said. 'I'd better be on my way.'

'Where are you off to next, then?' I said, and Dorothy said it was her friend Rose.

'I've been promising to visit Rose for months,' she said, 'but she cries all the time and it can become tedious.'

'Why does she cry all the time?' I said (thinking it was probably because Dorothy had just turned up, out of the blue, with her full set of luggage and all set for a long haul).

'I don't know,' said Dorothy. 'I've never been a crier myself.'

'Don't you ask her?'

'Oh no, never. Then I'd really be in for it.'

I helped her downstairs with her suitcase, and stood waving off the car. I watched until it vanished round the corner, and although

I was relieved she was gone, I felt strangely empty. It was Friday night. The shops all had their shutters down and the street was empty except for a couple getting money out of the cash machine. In the Victoria Bar a man was singing a Karaoke version of Meatloaf's 'Paradise on the Dashboard'.

I went upstairs and watched a documentary called *You Spoiled My Looks!* and then I went to bed.

I never saw Dorothy again. She died about a year later of a stroke. We put an announcement of her death in the local paper, and phoned up names we'd found in her address book. The funeral was well attended. I met Rose, the crier, who lived up to her reputation and wept bewilderedly throughout the service; and Clair and Alan Black, both luxuriously fat and dull, who seemed embarrassed and only stayed for half an hour at the hotel afterwards. Mum rushed around, perturbed because the sandwiches and tea still hadn't appeared.

I had thought Isobel might turn up. I had imagined her eating her breakfast, skimming over the newspaper and the announcement of Dorothy's death catching her eye. She would be startled, and drop her spoon. She would slip into the church, unnoticed (except by me) and listen quietly to the service. She wouldn't tell her husband she was going, she wouldn't announce herself to anyone. She would listen, and think back to herself and Dorothy in the dress shop, with the blinds pulled down, talking into the night.

But, of course, no Isobel turned up. And if she had, what would it have proved anyway? What difference would it have made?

Neighbours

Rose and Steven have been invited over to dinner by their new neighbours across the close. It was Rose who had been asked, a few days before, by Myra when they were both coming out of their front doors. Myra said it was nice to have some young people around. She would have a little soireé. They hadn't spoken before and the invitation was offered with so little ceremony or preamble that Rose was taken aback and hadn't time to think of an excuse. When she told Steven he said he wasn't bothered either way. Rose, trying vigorously to check her dread, kept saying it would be interesting.

'It'll be an experience,' she said. 'A sort of initiation into married life.'

For the last two days it was all she thought about. She was scared to meet Myra on the stairs and be forced to use up some of her conversational reserves. They had heard people come and go from Myra's flat, heard their voices, loud and theatrical, shouting *Ta ta, Cheeribye*, as if desperate to make their presence felt. (Once a woman's voice drifted up asserting she'd had a splendiferous time.) Rose imagined these people to be overblown and smug, quite certain of their opinions, vociferous in their dismissals or approvals. They knew their stake in life.

Steven said they sounded like oddities. This was a descriptive, rather than evaluative, term to him. He found most of the world odd and unfathomable, including Rose. His dealings with people were marked by amused, gentle patience.

Rose told him he shouldn't use that word. *Oddities*. She said it had bad connotations, and Steven said, 'But I love oddities.'

*

It's eight o'clock and Steven's still not ready. He's trimming his beard, dissatisfied with the way it's shaping up. He's discovered some sparseness in the chin region. Rose has been attempting to hurry him. At first she tried being calm and persistent, and then thunderously angry. Neither worked. When she comes into the bathroom, he says, 'Look at your big dour physiognomy. If the wind changes it'll stay that way and then you'll be in trouble.'

He slows down all his actions to an even more leisurely pace, looking up at Rose with his face upturned, covered in soap. His eyes are full of light, the very palest shade of chestnut, and they express laughter and glee, even when he's not laughing or gleeful. Rose smiles. She urges him again to hurry up, but without conviction now. He won't hurry, especially if she asks him. He'll make a stand. He kisses the top of her nose and says he's only joking, he's very fond of her big dour physiognomy.

'Less of the chat and more of the ablutions,' she says.

She checks herself in the mirror again. She isn't sure what is appropriate to wear to a *soirée*, or how much make-up to put on.

'Do you think they'll be nervous?' she says to Steven. Then, without pausing for a reply she says, 'Probably not. They invited us, after all. It'd be nice to be like that. To have people coming in and out of your house all the time, nothing formal. Easy come, easy go. It's kind of bohemian and free, don't you think?'

'I suppose,' says Steven. 'If you're that way inclined.'

'I never could be,' says Rose.

Myra swings the door open and begins to talk as if she's resuming an earlier conversation. Although this should be comforting, it's not. She talks as if she's some distance away and unaware of who she's talking to. Her long green dress swoops low at her chest, and her bare feet roll from side to side. Although she's only as tall as Rose's shoulder, there is something impressive and intimidating about her, authority in each of her tiny, considered movements. Her face would look glorious in a black-and-white photograph, the way it dips in and out of shadow and is not tempered with any female softness but shut up in itself, inviolate. Rose is disconcerted by her. She feels she could say something foolish and be disapproved of.

They walk through a long hallway with strings of flowers painted along the wall. Myra designed them herself.

'And there's a hummingbird,' she says, 'and two Birds of Paradise. I don't know if they're real birds or not, are they? I think they're flowers.'

'Oh, I don't know either,' says Rose. 'That's funny, isn't it?' She puts her hands in the air in a sort of nervous apology, and then drops them again. 'It's terrible how little I know about wildlife,' she says. 'Living in the city, I suppose.'

'No matter,' says Myra. 'They're my favourite birds whether they exist or not.'

In the living room, a man gets up from a big red futon to meet them. He takes Rose's hand and says, 'Who's this delightful personage?'

Myra tells him it's the neighbours. 'Remember, I told you?' she says.

'So you did. Pleased to make your acquaintance. I'm Tom, and I'll be your host for tonight.'

Steven hands him the beer and wine they've brought, *We come bearing gifts*, and Tom says they can definitely come again. Myra goes into the kitchen to get drinks, and Tom asks them how they're settling in, and then makes a few jokes about newly-weds. Rose is embarrassed, and glad when he starts talking about his job teaching philosophy at the university. He obviously expects to be liked and has no defences, no reservations about taking them into his confidence. However fraudulent this feeling of comradeship may be, Rose is grateful, feels almost privileged. He tells them about the bickering in his department, its banality and petty vindictiveness. With a hint of a boast he says they are trying to oust him, but that the students love him.

'Why are they trying to oust you?' says Rose.

'Misdemeanours,' he says, and when he goes on to say more, Myra cuts in and says that the less said about that the better.

'Political correctness gone mad,' says Tom.

Rose, embarrassed, says she believes in political correctness. She thinks it's a good thing that people are made aware, more aware, of the words they use, the implications behind certain words. Isn't political correctness only saying that all human beings should be treated with the same respect?

She sees Steven looking at her, smiling.

'Oh, to be young and idealistic,' says Myra, although Rose thinks she must only be in her early thirties. There is something tense and watchful about the way she sits forward all the time.

'I'll always believe that,' says Rose, 'no matter what age I am.'

Tom, who seems to have been waiting to resume the floor, roars, 'Anyway, the students would rally if that day ever came.'

Myra says that's the case. He bribes them by doing utterly outrageous and silly things, things that make them laugh. On the last day of term he burns a philosophy book in front of the whole class.

Tom cuts in and says, 'I quote Hume. *Any books containing divinity or metaphysics, commit to the flames: for they can contain nothing but sophistry and illusion.* I try and rotate them,' he says, 'so as not to be partial. Descartes is a popular choice, though.'

'The fire alarm always goes off,' says Myra, 'and he always gets into trouble. We loved it though.' After a pause she says, 'That's how we met. I was one of Tom's students. I had to leave, of course, after we started seeing each other.'

'She fell for my teaching prowess,' says Tom.

'Did you want to leave?' asks Rose.

Myra says it was just the way it was. Tom would have lost his job otherwise. After that she tried a few jobs, but none of them were suitable. She couldn't get on with the work, she couldn't get on with the people. She became a professional housewife.

'I do a bit of pottery,' she says, and shrugs. 'Some ceramics and watercolours. It's all very ladylike.'

Rose, looking between them, now notices how much older Tom is. He has a type of look she recognizes from pictures of Hemingway, the unbrushed sticking-out hair, an expansive, excessive chest. He looks incompetent in an entirely admirable way – as if he wouldn't be able to put on a pillowcase or iron a shirt. He would be chopping wood or fishing in treacherous waters. Although of course he wouldn't. He would be reading academic papers or struggling to finish a novel, and would never have been good at sport in school.

Tom asks them where they work, and Rose describes the old folks' home. She is pleased with her rendition of the manicness of the place, the good-natured battles between patients and staff that have a Carry-On aspect to them. Steven, who only talks when he's spoken to, tells them he designs and fits windows.

'See, like those windows,' he says, pointing, 'they've been done shoddily. Not a good job at all. The corners, see.' He shakes his head regretfully. 'I find myself looking at windows all the time when I shouldn't,' he says.

Myra says it sounds a strange job and Steven says not really, you make a good living.

'Up in the sky all day,' he says, 'closer to God.'

Tom says he hopes they don't have a Christian amongst them.

They drink gin and tonics and beers. Myra brings the drinks in from the kitchen, the bottles balancing precariously on a sort of trolley.

'It's my hostess trolley,' she says. 'I found it in a junk shop.'

'That kitsch stuff's coming into fashion again, isn't it?' says Rose. '*Abigail's Party* kind of vibe.'

Sometimes, when they're having some stuffy professor couple round to dinner, Myra wears a pair of leopardskin stilettos she has, and her lycra slut dress, and she totters in pushing her hostess trolley. She and Tom pretend it's nothing out of the ordinary. They pretend they think it's classy.

'But I couldn't be bothered tonight,' says Myra.

Steven asks if anyone minds if he rolls a joint and Tom says to go ahead, he could do with a smoke. He gets out his accoutrements and sets about making it, his face furled with childish intent.

'It's good weed,' he says, 'Moroccan. Have a sniff,' and he passes it over to Tom.

'He gets it from the boy who works on the Co-op deli counter,' says Rose. 'Half a block of Double Gloucester and a quarter-ounce of skunk.'

She is embarrassed by Steven's enthusiasm for drugs, his drug stories. When they first started going out he was always telling her about his LSD trip. How the grapes disengaged themselves from the wallpaper and pinged off his nose. He is a timid person, with a strong sense of self-preservation, and she's never believed he actually took it. He is intensely attuned to the workings of his body, the peregrinations of blood, of vitamins, of pains that start gently and swell to potential throat cancer, burst eardrums, melanoma. It annoys Rose sometimes. A lot of things about Steven are starting to frustrate her, and to make her feel lonely, and then guilty. A few times he has come back from work and found her crying. He puts his arms around her and says, 'It's okay, I'm home now.' And then all her feelings of frustration and loneliness and guilt compound together and make her feel dreadful, monstrous. She has told him she is a bad person and will probably have to be put down.

Myra goes into the kitchen for a while and brings out some food. There's toasted bread with crushed sun-dried tomatoes, and a bowl of humous and pitta bread, and a bean salad. There are a couple of hand-painted plates with big hunks of broken dark chocolate on them. Myra says to help themselves. Those formal dinner parties with everyone sitting grimly round a table make her want to puke. Tom congratulates her on her fine purvey, a veritable Babette's Feast, and they begin to eat. Outside, patches of tangerine sky show through big grey clouds, and the room is shadowy, lit by two standard lamps with tasselled Chinese scarves. Rose, with the help of the gin, begins to feel more comfortable. She notices that Myra looks almost exclusively at Tom. She looks at him like she's ready to be amused and delighted by anything he has to say. Sometimes she nods her head slightly, egging him on. Tom does most of the talking. He's the ringmaster, Myra his beautiful assistant, and she and Steven the enthralled spectators. He tells them about a book he's writing, a kind of class handbook that whizzes through centuries of philosophical thought. It's going to be full of jokes and irreverent anecdotes, and get up the noses of academics. Rose asks him who his favourite philosopher is, and he says he likes the existentialists, little Sartre and his chums. He says Kierkegaard's a real crackpot too. For Rose, there is something shocking and thrilling about the way he talks so casually about the leviathans of philosophy, as if he thinks them all absurd, tame eccentrics. It's an impressive mark of his learning, she thinks, to be able to talk so. She says she thinks she's an existentialist too. Her favourite authors are Albert Camus and Simone de Beauvoir. Myra says she's a Hobbesian.

'What's that?'

Myra says it's a theory that says everyone's out to get what they want, everyone's selfish.

'That's interesting,' says Rose, 'but I don't agree. People do good things all the time. Like saving someone from a fire, things that they do on the spur of the moment, not thinking about themselves.'

'But saving someone from a fire makes *them* feel good,' says Myra. 'It gives *them* a warm glow.'

'No,' says Rose again. She wishes she had time to go home and think about it and then come back with her arguments in order. 'Some acts are selfless,' she says, 'like one of your desires can be to make other people happy.'

But instead of answering, Myra smiles and shakes her head, as if saying this is finished, I'm bored.

'What about you, Steven?' says Tom. 'What are you?'

He's sitting right back in the sofa, his legs sprawled apart, and smiling benignly, with sweet, lazy assurance. 'I'm a human bean,' he says.

They all laugh, and Tom says that's the best answer. Rose wishes she'd thought of it.

Myra puts on a Leonard Cohen CD and they pass around another joint. Rose talks about an article she read about him, and they talk about music they like, books they like. She notices that Myra seems surprised that she knows a lot about different authors, and how she looks at her with new interest. She feels elated under their attention, in her element. She says that it's good to have people to talk to about books; the only thing Steven reads is Horatio Hornblower stories.

'I've never heard of them,' says Myra. 'Who are they by?'

Steven tells her they're boys' adventure stories. Really funny, he says.

They put on more records and drink more gin. Myra's the only one of them who doesn't seem to be drunk. Tom is beginning to slur his words, his face flushed, and his conversation getting louder, more demanding. He wants to know what happiness is, what would make them happy. Myra groans and says no party games. Certainly no philosophy party games.

'Shh,' he says. 'Let them answer. Steven?' he says.

'I'm stoned, I can't think.' Then he says, 'You know when you take butter straight from the fridge and put it on bread? It makes me happy when the bread doesn't break.'

When it's Rose's turn to answer she doesn't know what to say. She is angry at being put in the position, of being looked at, almost aggressively, by Tom. At the same time, it seems important that she thinks about it, that it is a serious question, that this is a *real* conversation.

'I don't know,' she says.

'That's not good enough.'

'Tom, just leave it,' says Myra.

Rose says she doesn't know what would make her happy, she's destined to be a malcontent. She says to Myra, 'What do you think?'

Myra says that when she was growing up her mother didn't like her. She says this matter-of-factly, as if she's describing a table or a blade of grass. Her mother just didn't take to her, and Myra didn't get on with other children. She thought they were loud and frightening and calamitous. So she made up imaginary friends.

'They were more imaginary adversaries,' says Myra. 'They used to chase me round the garden.'

She was always looking for an ideal friend, even when she was an adult, and then she met Tom.

'And he's my ideal friend,' she says, 'so I suppose he makes me happy.' She gets up and says, 'Well, that's my turn over, I'm going to the toilet.'

When she leaves the room, there's silence for a few minutes. Tom seems unaffected, as if he's heard it all before, and he opens another beer, offers it around. Rose asks where the kitchen is; she needs a glass of water.

The kitchen is just the kind of kitchen she would like. There's a huge shiny cooker that takes up half the counter. All the jumble, the crockery and cooking utensils, the herbs and spices, a row of cactuses, are colourful and homely, lackadaisically arranged to just the right effect. She thinks what a strange and alluring life Myra and Tom lead.

She splashes her face with water and dries herself on a tea towel. She goes over to the sink and runs the tap again. When she hears someone come in, she knows it's Tom. She doesn't know how she knows, or why she doesn't turn round. He doesn't say anything but walks over to the sink, behind her. He puts a hand on her breast. At first she thinks it's a mistake. She thinks he's trying to reach for something on the draining board and he's brushed past her accidentally. It happens in a split second. She pushes him away with her elbow.

'You must have thought I was Myra,' she says lightly.

But when she looks around, Tom doesn't say anything. He's staring at her, and he's laughing. He's not making any sound, but he's laughing.

Rose goes back into the living room where Myra and Steven are sitting. After a few minutes she says, 'I think I've had too much to drink. We'd better go home. Steven.'

'The night's young,' he says. 'Have some coffee or something.'

'No, really. I think I'd better go now.'

No matter how hard she stares at Steven, he makes no attempt to rouse himself. Tom comes back into the room and asks who wants another drink.

'Not us,' says Rose, 'we're just leaving. Steven,' she says, 'get up.'

Myra is looking at Tom, then Rose, looking between them. Not moving, she says, 'It's late, they should probably leave.'

'Steven can stay,' says Tom. 'Let him have his say.'

'I'd better go with the little lady,' says Steven.

Back in the flat Rose says, 'What was that about, *the little lady*?'

'I was only joking. Lighten up, Rose.'

He makes toasted cheese and they sit on the sofa. 'I suppose you'll want to talk about it,' he says, smiling and stroking her hair. 'What are your thoughts?'

'Nothing. It was awful.'

He says he had a good time. 'That Myra's a bit of a cold fish, though,' he says. 'I liked him.'

'I didn't like him,' says Rose. 'I thought she was more interesting. She's sort of funny, like his moll or something. I don't want to see them again.'

Steven says she's so contrary. He thought they were exactly the kind of people she would like, all the talk about books and philosophy and that.

'It was awful,' she says again.

She lies against him on the settee, and soon feels his muscles relax, his body go limp in preparation for sleep. She used to wonder if he never thought about things or if he did think about things, but kept silent about them. She sees it differently now. She sees that he is not disturbed by life in the way she is. It does not present a challenge to him.

'Steven?'

'What?' He turns his head towards her, nearly asleep.

And, looking at his calm, imperturbable face, she can form no words. Where would she start?

'Nothing, sorry. Go back to sleep.'

Renaissance

My mum was generally a cheerful person. It was her misfortune that she had borne a child who was neither cheerful, nor endowed with finer feelings, as she was. She was always telling me that when I was a baby I used to lie completely quiet and still for hours and people would say to her, 'Are you sure that baby's alive?' and sometimes she herself wondered. She couldn't understand it because she came from a family of lookers-on-the-bright-side. It was in the genes.

'Our family motto,' she said, 'was if you break a leg, just be thankful you didn't break two legs.'

We only went up to Granny Philips's twice a year, and I never found her and Grandpa very cheery. There was plastic covering the sofa and tables, and the only time they smiled was when their dog, Gertrude, came into the room. The conversation revolved around Gertrude – they loved her more than they loved each other – and Sam, Mum's brother, who had depression, and still lived at home.

'You *think* you've got depression,' Mum would say to him, 'but answer me this. Do people in Africa have depression? Do they have time to get depressed when they've got to walk to the well and work in the fields? Can they just stay in bed all day, watching cartoons and thinking how miserable they are?'

'I suppose not,' Sam would say, slumped in his seat, looking more and more depressed.

Mum's one beef was that she never went to university. This was the only subject that was immune to her abrasive brand of looking on the bright side. If she had gone, she said, she would have studied English. She had won a prize at school for an essay entitled 'Why We Read'. She could remember whole poems, and could recite them off by heart to prove it. One of them was 'The Donkey' by Chesterton. For this one she adopted a low, sad voice, and stood rooted to the spot as if she were possessed by the spirit of the donkey. When it came to *Fools! For I also had my hour* she would fairly belt the line out. I disliked these performances. I found them sentimental, and never knew what to say when she had finished and was looking at me with such sad triumph. Once I asked her what happened to the donkey afterwards, and she got annoyed and said he just went back to being an ugly donkey, but that that wasn't the point.

Mum cited my dad as the reason she didn't go to university. She said she would have thrived in such an atmosphere, but that he didn't want her thriving. He wanted a good little doctor's wife. Dad said the real reason was that Mum didn't have the qualifications to get into university, and that having a good head for poetry didn't mean she was brainy anyway. It just meant she had a good memory. This was the one thing he could say that truly enraged Mum. Usually she ignored his drunken rants, the rants where he would call everyone he knew rotten bastards and elaborate endlessly on the ways they had wronged him. But she couldn't let a slur on her intelligence pass by without comment.

'I'm not the one who had to re-sit their exams three times,' she'd say.

Other times she'd mention her IQ, or the fact that Dad had been scared to try a tomato until he was twenty-one, or that he'd only ever read one book in his life. She never mentioned the most obvious thing, that he was killing off what was left of his brain with alcohol. She ignored what she didn't want to face, and made it seem somehow bad-mannered to mention the obvious. So I never mentioned it either.

I spent most of my time with Mum, and didn't see Dad very much. He worked late, and often wouldn't be home until I'd gone to bed. My response to him was complicated by the fact that he was so changeable. When he was sober he was gentle and easy to be with. We would play draughts or chess together, or take a walk to the beach and skim pebbles. He didn't talk very much and was more comfortable showing me how to do things. By the time I was nine I could put someone in the recovery position, wire a plug, and tie knots to shame the Boy Scouts. Dad never talked about his life, but I felt he was sad, and when he was sober I felt sorry for him. He had a doleful, refugee look about him, as if he didn't belong with the people around him and was ready to apologize at any moment for his presence. I never thought about him being a doctor, and I was always surprised at Christmas time when he would bring home presents his patients had given him. (Unfortunately it was mostly bottles of whisky, which meant a lot of Xmas cheer for Dad, and not much for Mum and me). For a little while his black bag with his medical equipment inside – his props, Dad called them – fascinated me. The props looked so alien and authoritative, yet Dad could wield them and interpret their signals. When I asked him about them he explained what they were used for, and said they were easy to handle once you knew how.

'Anyone can do it,' he said, and I believed him and stopped being impressed.

By the time I was twelve he was drunk or hung over more often than he was sober. One afternoon, just before the summer holidays, Mum came into my room and told me we were moving.

'Your father's lost his job,' she said. 'He's in disgrace.'

'What'd he do?' I said.

Mum walked over to the window and stared outside. Then she came over and put her hands on my shoulders.

'Don't hunch,' she said, 'it makes you look like an old woman.'

'I'm not hunching,' I said.

She said it would be good for us to live somewhere new, but she didn't sound as if she believed it.

'You'll miss your friends,' she said, 'but you'll make new ones. And so will I. It'll be exciting.'

'I don't have any friends,' I said, which was true.

'Well, that's even better then,' she said, 'you won't miss anyone. I'll tell you what I'll miss. I'll miss Lucy, and I'll miss the book group –'

I interrupted to remind her that she didn't even like the book group, and when she denied it I cited the week before when she told me they weren't a very bright bunch, and all they wanted to do was gossip and read Joanna Trollope novels.

'I did not say that,' said Mum, 'and even if I did, it doesn't mean I won't miss them. When I think of them discussing *Pride and Prejudice* without me . . . I have a lot to say about that book,' she added ominously.

I said I was sure they'd miss her too, and Mum surprised me by smiling hesitantly and saying, 'Do you think they will?'

It was on the tip of my tongue to say, *No, they'll crack open the party poppers*, but I looked at her face and said, 'Of course they'll miss you. You're the life and soul of that book group.'

'I'm sure that's not true,' she said, in a way that made me believe she thought it was very true indeed, 'but it's very nice of you to say so.'

She went on for another ten minutes about what she'd miss – the beach, the house, the weather – until she stopped and said there must be *something* I'd miss.

'I don't know yet,' I said. 'I won't know until we're gone.'

I saw her looking at me, willing me to mention something we could share together.

'I might miss the tree,' I said, 'in the front garden.'

'Oh, the tree!' she said in sudden delight. 'I love that tree. When you were little, you and I used to sit under that tree for hours in the summertime. You used to stare up at the leaves and there wouldn't be a peep out of you. I used to wonder what you were thinking, you looked so serious for a baby.'

'I was probably thinking I wish Mum wouldn't stick me under this stupid tree for hours,' I said, and Mum laughed.

'And there was me,' she said, 'thinking you were deep.'

It was an eternal disappointment to her that I wasn't deep, as she had hoped, but just quiet. Mum's criteria for deepness were pretty arbitrary anyway – they involved liking poetry and crying at sad films, as she did. I scuppered my chances of ever being deep by laughing during the graveyard scene in *Who Will Love My Children*.

'Anyway,' she said, 'we'll be together, you and me. That's what matters.'

'And Dad,' I said, but Mum kissed the back of my head and didn't say anything to that.

We arrived in Glasgow one rainy Friday night, two days into my summer holidays. Mum said Glasgow meant dear green place, but it didn't look very green. We passed groups of dark high-rise flats, shabby rows of shops, huge billboard stands. A fat girl behind the counter of a fish-and-chip shop stuck her two fingers up at me as we waited at the traffic lights.

'Would you look at that,' said Mum, 'she must be very unhappy.'

But the girl didn't look unhappy at all. She looked like she wanted to bash someone, preferably me. When I said this to Mum, she replied that my outlook on life was superficial.

'Any psychologist worth his salt will tell you,' she said, 'that behind every bully is a very scared, very sad person.'

I rolled my eyes and looked out of the window. It had begun to strike me, in the past year, that Mum could be a bit dim. It wouldn't matter, I thought, if she wasn't so pleased with herself.

'I agree with Cara,' Dad said suddenly. It startled me to hear his voice because I'd forgotten he was there. What can you say to someone who agrees with you? I said nothing and we rolled into Waver Street in silence.

The delivery van arrived the next morning, and we spent the next few days unpacking. The house was too small for all our things, and we had to start piling stuff into cupboards. The first things to go were Mum's pictures, which looked wrong on the murky, floral walls. Then old photo albums, vases, toiletry sets, my old christening gown, her old christening gown. Hoarding was the one indulgence Mum allowed herself. She never threw anything away without a wrench of her heart. She got nostalgic about an old clay bear she'd made at school, and angry and disappointed reading my old school reports, which, apart from maths which Mum didn't rate anyway, were roundly bad. One entry particularly incensed her for its inelegance and atrocious spelling:

Cara may be a good student if she paid atention in class. As it is, she pays no attention, and is not a good student.

'She certainly didn't beat around the bush,' Mum said. We were sitting on the living-room floor, the papers scattered around us.

'They all say the same,' she said. 'Why do you think that is?' She gave me a concentrated look, as if my answer was the most important thing in the whole world. I hated that look.

'I don't know,' I said and shrugged. 'Because I don't pay attention?'

From upstairs came the sound of Dad laughing. I'd taken his lunch up to their room earlier and he'd been watching a Jerry Springer show about people who wanted to marry their pets. He'd pointed to the telly with his vodka bottle and said it just wasn't right to get engaged to your horse.

'Well,' said Mum sharply, 'you'll need to start paying attention. You're going into second year after the summer, that's when the wheat's separated from the chaff. I want to see you in the wheat pile.'

I said what if I liked it in the chaff pile, and Mum said to stop being facetious. 'Stupidness doesn't suit anyone,' she said.

This brought on a reverie about her own thwarted ambition, what she could have excelled in (anything she wanted!) if she'd been given the chances and opportunities I had.

'I just soaked up knowledge,' she said. 'I was thankful for it. How many other people,' she said, 'can recite the whole of "Hail to thee blithe spirit! Bird that never wert" off by heart?'

That same day, Mum decided we should introduce ourselves to

the neighbours. Only one woman answered our knock, and we had to call out our business before she would open the door.

'I thought you were those Jehovah Witnesses,' she said.

'Oh no,' said Mum. 'Though hopefully we bring good news,' she added in an excruciatingly jolly voice.

Shelia was round and solid as a Christmas pudding. Her t-shirt said FCUK OFF although her expression alone conveyed this message. I was intimidated by her, but also impressed by the short thrift she gave Mum.

'Well, hen, I'm busy,' she said after a few minutes, practically shutting the door in our faces. I'd never seen Mum dismissed before: she was used to regimenting people's emotional responses to match her own.

'Not a congenial person at all,' Mum said when we got home.

'Behind every bully is a very scared, very sad person,' I said, pleased with myself.

We saw Shelia again a few nights later. She came to the door late on Saturday night to tell Mum that Dad was passed out at the bottom of the street. At first Mum tried to pretend she didn't know what Shelia was talking about. This was pretty futile, as Dad had been sitting in the garden for the past two days saluting everyone who went past.

'Well, he must have a twin,' said Shelia, 'and it's conked out down the road.'

'Okay, well thank you for letting us know,' said Mum brightly.

We went down the road to get him. He had a cut down one side of his face, and was muttering something about shitheads. Mum gave him a hanky for his face, but he groggily swiped it away.

'You! What do you care?' he said, slurring his words.

'We both care,' I said, desperate to get him off the street.

'She doesn't. She wouldn't spit on me if I was on fire.'

'Don't be ridiculous,' said Mum. 'Grab his other arm, Cara.'

'You'd probably laugh your head off,' he said, a note of girlish hysteria creeping into his voice. 'You'd have a ball!'

I tried to lift his arm to pull him up, but it was no use. He was too heavy and making no attempt to help us. He stumbled up himself, calling us a couple of fuckers before he lurched away.

Things got back to normal pretty quickly. Dad got a job, I don't know how he managed it, working in a doctor's surgery in Bearsden. His drinking eased up, and became confined to frantic, demented bouts of one or two days. We hardly noticed him except when he was drunk. It was like realizing you had a ghost only when you heard its manacles rattle. Sometimes he would come into my room. He always used a pretext: he wanted to seal my window, bleed the radiator. He would hang around afterwards and maybe say something like: 'That was five flus today. There's something going around.'

'Mmm,' I'd say.

'Have you been feeling okay? No temperature, no aches and pains?'

'Nope.'

'Good.' He would muse on this quietly for a few minutes. Then he would get up and say, 'Well, tell me if you feel anything coming on.'

A month after we moved in he came in to show me a big card everyone had signed for his birthday. He pointed out all the names and told me what job each of them did at the surgery. Everyone had written a message, which he read out in embarrassed pleasure.

'They all call you Teddy,' I said. 'Not William?'

'I know,' said Dad. 'That's their nickname for me.'

He told me that the last time he'd had a nickname was at school. The boys in his class called him walnut face, because of his acne. But, as Dad pointed out, that wasn't really a nickname.

'That was just people being cruel,' he said.

Later that night I asked Mum if she'd seen the card. We were side by side at the sink, Mum washing, me drying. She was humming a tune and broke off, smiling at me as if she'd just realized I was there.

'The card,' I said, 'did you see it?'

'Of course I saw it,' she said. 'It was very nice.'

'He seems quite popular,' I said, handing her back a plate with a tomato sauce stain. It was one of her principles to be sloppy about housework.

'Yes, people always take to your father. He has a very modest way about him, people like that.'

'Is that why you liked him?' I asked, and Mum said she supposed it must have been.

'It's so long ago now,' she said. 'I was just turned eighteen when we got married. You don't know your own mind at that age. All I wanted was to be grown-up, have a house, a husband, a big wedding. Idiotic,' she said, 'that was just the word for me at that age.'

She smiled fondly at the thought of her younger, idiotic self, and went back to humming her tune.

If anything, Mum was happier after we moved to Glasgow. She joined a hill-walking club and went on jaunts with them every Saturday. She came back late in the evening, full of the joys. Scotland had the most beautiful scenery – she described it rapturously – and the people in the group were the most interesting and well-informed people you could hope to meet.

'It's so invigorating,' she said after the first meeting, 'to meet people who understand you. People you can talk to.'

'Are they all loonies too, then?' I said, but Mum was in a good mood and just laughed.

I got to know everyone in the hill-walking group on a first name basis. Velma, a retired schoolteacher, wonderful for her age, but you didn't want to get stuck as her partner because her arthritis slowed her down considerably. Gina and Tom, the couple who got on well, and Clair and Philip, who didn't. Betty the librarian, who didn't seem interested when Mum tried to engage her on the subject of literature. The person she talked most about, though, was a divorcee called Brian. He taught a communication course in a college in Hamilton, and his life had been a life compounded of misfortune. His parents died in a car crash, his sister was a recovering drug-addict, his ex-wife a jealous psychotic.

'But he doesn't let life get him down,' said Mum, admiration shining through her voice. 'He just refuses.'

He revealed his life to her on these walks, supposedly because she was a good listener, and empathetic to boot. He said these were rare qualities.

We finished the dishes, and Mum dried her hands and said she'd better get ready. She was meeting the hill-walking group in the pub at seven.

'That's the second time this week you're going out,' I said. 'Not including Saturday.'

Mum said she was in the house all day with me, wasn't she allowed to see her friends at night? 'Humans are social animals,' she said, 'they need other people to spark off.'

'For hearty outdoor types, you spend a lot of time in the pub,' I said.

'I don't know why you're being like this. You've got Barbara now. I don't stop you seeing her.'

In fact, I wished Mum would stop me seeing Barbara. She was someone I was scared *not* to be friends with. She was thirteen, a year older than me, and none of the other girls in the street would hang around with her. Barbara said it was because they were snobs, but the real reason was that she hit them. I didn't know if she hit them because they didn't like her, or if they didn't like her because she hit them. The thing was that Barbara insisted on being involved in everything they were doing. There were four girls, all about our ages, that lived in Waver Street. When it was hot, as it had been for weeks, they spread blankets on the street and lounged around on them. They read magazines, painted each other's nails, plaited their hair with beads. Barbara was bony, with a greyish, old-china tinge to her skin. She had heavy, greasy black hair, thick eyebrows, and a huge nose that she often stroked self-consciously. She didn't look like the kind of girl who could get away with thinking she was pretty, or worth decorating.

The first time I met her was one of those hot days. I was sitting with the girls, whose names I'd instantly forgotten, trying to decide how I could escape home without seeming rude. I was going through what Mum called a beefy stage, and I towered above them in height and girth. They were asking each other questions from a 'How Good A Friend Are You?' quiz in a magazine. Barbara came along and stood beside the blanket.

'Ask me,' she said fiercely, halfway between a threat and a plea. One of the girls, a bossy, vicious blonde, said, 'Why, Barbara? You don't have any friends.'

'I do so,' said Barbara. 'And they're better than any of you.'

'Unless you count her nits,' another girl said, and they all tittered.

'I don't have nits,' Barbara said flatly. 'You have nits.'

'Very clever,' said the blonde one. 'How long did it take you to think that one up, Barbara?'

They all ignored her after that, but Barbara kept standing there. And then suddenly she swooped down and walloped one of them on the face. The girls jumped apart, shouting, but not before Barbara had managed to rain a few more blows on them. It all lasted only a few minutes. Barbara stopped abruptly and walked away, giving me a half-hearted push on her way past.

A few days later I was down at the disused railway line at the back of Waver Street. I was walking up and down the tracks, bored, when Barbara appeared.

'Hey you,' she said, 'what's your name?'

'Cara,' I said.

'What kind of name's that?' she said, and I shrugged. She sat at the edge of the platform and swung her legs over the edge.

'Everyone says your dad's an alkie,' she said.

'He's not. He's a doctor.'

'Doesn't matter anyway. They say things about me, too, that aren't true. They make me so mad.'

'I'd better go,' I said after a few minutes of silence.

She was picking a scab on her knee and didn't look up. 'See you around,' she said as I walked away.

*

Barbara was very definite about what she wanted to do, and more and more she wanted me to accompany her while she did it. Even though I didn't like her, it never occurred to me to say no to her. At first we just walked around the streets. Then Barbara started to invite me to her house. The curtains were never open, but the sun shone through them and showed up dust everywhere. There were ashtrays, and old newspapers, and dirty plates and cups lying around; a smell of old cat-food permeated the house. Barbara's room was the worst. There were clothes all over the floor, mixed up with plates and bowls crusted with dried-on food. A box of cereal with cornflakes spilling out of it lay in the corner of her room for weeks. The only things that Barbara took care of were her old, beat-up trumpet, and her cassette player. She had two tapes – Simply Red and Louis Armstrong – and she made us listen to them right through, in total silence. The other thing she liked to do was rifle through her mum's bedroom. She would pull all her clothes out of the wardrobe, onto the bed, and run her hands tenderly through them, as if she were touching skin.

'Has your mum got this many clothes?' she asked me once.

I didn't know what to say: her mum's clothes were cheap and pretty ordinary looking. I couldn't understand their appeal.

'I don't know,' I said. 'I suppose so.'

'One day I'm going to have even more than this.'

She held up a red, silky blouse, smelt it, and then passed it to me.

'That's the perfume she wears,' she said. 'It costs thirty-two pounds, and that's just for a tiny bottle.'

It was in her mum's bedroom that she showed me the photographs. She got them out of a drawer where they'd been hidden under piles of underwear. They were of normal size, bad quality. A woman bending over and spreading her bum cheeks; lying on her back with her legs splayed; on all fours like a dog. On and on. Barbara looked at each of them carefully, seriously, before passing them to me. Someone was playing a radio outside, and apart from that it was deadly quiet.

'Why's your mum got these?' I said at last.

'They're of her, stupid.'

'They're disgusting,' I said, and Barbara said, 'I know,' and gathered them up and hid them away again.

A few days later I met her mum for the first time. I was sitting in Barbara's room, listening to her practise her trumpet. She couldn't play a note on it; she just blew into it as hard as she could and wiggled her fingers about. She told me that the best musicians in the world were self-taught. We heard the front door open, and then someone's feet coming up the stairs. Barbara stopped and shouted, 'Mum?'

'You don't need to holler like that, Barbara,' said her mum. She stood in the doorway, a dumpy, baggy woman wearing jeans and a denim jacket. Her brown hair was tied in a ponytail, and she had a weary, fleshy face that looked like it couldn't be bothered to decide on an expression. She looked round the room blankly; she didn't say hello, or ask me my name, as all the mums I'd ever met did.

'Do you want to hear my trumpet, Mum?' said Barbara in a plaintive voice I'd never heard her use before.

'Not just now,' she sighed. 'I've got to go out again.'

I felt myself staring at her, and turned away. Trying to connect her with the woman in the photographs was like trying to imagine what ice-cream sprinkled with salt would taste like. Except more disturbing.

'Where're you going?' said Barbara.

'Phil's taking me out.'

She left and we heard her bedroom door close.

'You need to go now,' said Barbara, pushing me towards the door. 'I want to see my mum.'

I got home, relieved at how normal and orderly everything looked. The gate, the curtains pulled efficiently at either side of the window. They made Barbara's house seem a Gothic extravagance of my imagination, and my involvement in her life slipped away: I forgot her.

The kitchen door was open. I could hear Mum's voice. And

then a man's voice. They were at the kitchen table drinking tea.

'I ask you,' Mum was saying, 'whoever heard of Lady Macbeth urinating in the middle of the stage? And then the three witches wearing sunglasses! I nearly fell off my seat.'

'It's just shock value these days,' the man said. 'They want to grind your face in the shit, as Pinter said.'

'Oh,' said Mum, and paused. I could tell she didn't know who Pinter was. 'Just lamentable,' she said after a few seconds, 'that's what it was.'

'What was?' I said suddenly, walking into the kitchen. They hadn't noticed me and Mum was surprised.

'Well hello to you too,' she said. 'Cara, this is Brian from the group, Brian this is Cara.'

'Hello there,' he said.

'Hi.'

I walked over to the cupboard and got out a packet of crisps.

'Put those back,' Mum shouted over. 'It'll be lunch soon, I don't want you stuffing your face with rubbish.'

'I'm *starving*.'

'You don't look starving. Quite the opposite.'

I sat down at the table and Mum told me they were talking about the play they'd seen last night. I'd been asleep when she came in.

'To be fair,' said Brian, talking precisely as if he were picking insects from his food, 'the ending was good. It meant we got to go home.'

Mum flashed him a brilliant smile. 'That's right,' she said. 'And the seats,' she said, 'those little hard seats!'

'We should go to the pantomime next time,' Brian said, 'I bet you get a comfy seat there.'

Mum started talking about how she'd never been to the theatre until she was seventeen – 'It was *Death of a Salesman*,' she said. 'I just sat there, gripped' – and how she'd hardly been since because she had no one to go with.

'You've never invited me,' I said.

'That's because you wouldn't like it.'

She looked at me absent-mindedly and then directed her attention back to Brian. 'She'd fidget, like her dad. I took him to see *The Silver Darlings* once and he fidgeted the whole time. He only perked up when I bought him a Cornetto at the interval.'

Brian started talking about his ex-wife, the one Mum told me about who had tried to poison him and phoned him up late at night to screech at him. He didn't look the kind of man anyone would screech down the phone at. There was something well tended and carefully refined about him – his fine black sweater, gold-rimmed glasses, the considered smile on his face. A certain amount of woody aftershave floated around him and got up my nose.

Mum made us bacon and eggs for lunch. It took her ten minutes to notice I hadn't touched my bacon.

'What's wrong with it?' she said. 'Why aren't you eating?'

'You've given me all the fatty bits,' I said, looking down at my plate and pushing the bacon around with my fork.

'Don't be ridiculous,' she said.

I was angry and more upset than the situation warranted. I sat staring at the table until Mum cleared the plates away and said that it was up to me if I didn't want to eat it.

'Missing a meal won't kill you,' she said.

I never saw Brian after that, although Mum went out with him at night. He waited for her in his car, the engine purring. They still went hill-walking on Saturdays, and during the week there were poetry readings, plays, the foreign cinema, folk-singing evenings at the Scotia bar.

'Why don't you go along?' I said to Dad one night. He was sitting in the living room, reading the paper. Mum was getting changed in the bedroom.

'It's not really my cup of tea,' he said. 'I just get bored at that kind of thing.'

'You might like it,' I said. 'You won't know if you never go.'

'Who'd look after you?' he said, and I said I could look after myself. I wanted to say something about Brian, although I didn't know what. I didn't know how to say it.

'Do you want to try and beat me at chess?' Dad said.

'No thanks.'

'Scared I'll thrash you,' he said, tugging me gently on the arm. I was angry at him suddenly, angry because he seemed so piteous, so clumsy and needy in his affection.

'I just don't feel like it,' I said, and left the room.

During this period – I remember it as a few weeks, although it was probably longer – Mum was positively incandescent. She laughed all the time, she acted silly, thrilled at her own silliness, and spoke constantly about what she'd seen and done, and who said what to whom. She didn't speak about the old house any more, she said moving to Glasgow was the best decision she'd ever made. 'This is my renaissance,' she was fond of saying. She enrolled for an Open University course in English literature after the summer, and read through the brochures during dinner.

'Don't get your hopes up,' Dad said. 'You might find it too difficult. It's been years since you've had to write an essay.'

'I'll manage,' said Mum serenely. She was as untouched by him recently as a Buddha is untouched by worldly possessions. She ate her dinner, enchanted with whatever she was thinking about. When Dad told her about his day, she didn't even feign interest.

One night she never returned home. We'd bought my school uniform that afternoon. It was a week till the end of the school holidays. I'd woken up because Dad had fallen against the Welsh dresser, which banged off the wall.

'Is Mum not home yet?' I said, rubbing my eyes.

Dad shrugged and let his hands fall into his lap. 'She's old enough to look after herself,' he said. 'She'll be back.'

I stood at the window and looked out at the street. It was two in the morning. The street was empty and all the lights in the houses were off.

'Phone her friends,' I said, turning round to Dad. 'Ask them if they've seen her.'

'At least she has friends,' said Dad. He was holding his head in his hands as if it were a piece of precious, over-ripe fruit. 'You don't know what it's like,' he said. 'Loneliness. Having no one care about you. They say, they say you can't name things you can't see, but try loneliness. You can't see it, but it's there. It's in me.'

He patted his chest and shut his eyes very slowly and then opened them again.

'Try the soul,' he said.

I went through to the kitchen to look for her address book, but I couldn't find it. When I went back into the living room Dad was snoring. I emptied his vodka into the sink, and then stood at the window again. Still nothing. At some point I must have fallen asleep. I woke up on the couch the next morning. It took me a few minutes to remember something was wrong, and then I ran through the house, checking all the rooms. All her clothes were still there, everything she owned still there. I woke up Dad. He phoned the hospitals, police stations, all the people they knew in Dorset, Gran and Grandpa. No one knew anything. We couldn't find any numbers for the hill-walking group.

'We'll just have to wait,' said Dad.

A letter came for me the next day. I knew right away it was Mum's writing. Dad read it after me. He didn't say a word. Then he put his arms around me and said, 'I'm sorry, I'm so sorry.' I pushed him away and shouted that it was all his fault. I ripped the letter up, but later Dad Sellotaped it together and brought it up to my room.

'You might want to keep it,' he said, and put it down on my desk. And in the end, I did.

A few days later I was with Barbara. We were straddling the roof of a tenement flat, having climbed up the scaffolding on Barbara's insistence. It was windy and I grabbed onto the edge, terrified.

'I've not seen you for a while,' she said. She was hardly holding on at all. I shrugged and looked over the rooftops.

'I'm going to jump,' she said. She slid down the roof on her bum and disappeared. I shouted her name, but there was no reply. My voice echoed into the silence. I kept shouting, expecting her to reappear, but she didn't. I was scared to move and had to force myself to slide down. There was a narrow row of steel stairs scaling the building, and I went down them gingerly, my hands sweating. She was lying on the pavement, one arm flung out behind her head. I was crouched over her, screaming, when her eyes flew open and she began to laugh.

'Got you,' she said.

'That's not funny,' I said, walking away. I was still shaking.

'As if you'd care,' she said, 'if I was dead.' She looked at me out of the corners of her eyes as if she had asked me a question and was waiting for a reply.

'I would care,' I said, 'and so would your mum.'

'Shows how much you know,' said Barbara. She started walking alongside me.

'Would your mum care?' she asked me. She spoke in her usual flat voice, but she was looking at me slyly.

'Yeah, of course,' I said.

'Hmm,' said Barbara. 'I thought friends were meant to tell each other everything,' she said.

I stopped and stared at her. 'Well, you're not my friend,' I said. 'And I don't want to know your stupid secrets anyway. I don't want to go to your smelly house, and look at your smelly mum's photographs.'

'At least my mum doesn't abandon me,' Barbara shouted. 'Shows how much she loves you.'

'She does. I mean, she's not. Abandoned me, she's not.'

'Everyone knows. *Everyone*,' said Barbara in a quieter voice.

And the next thing I knew, I was hitting her as hard as I could. I gave her a black eye, but the next day she came to my door and acted as if nothing had happened.

'You okay?' she said.

'Yeah,' I said. 'You?'

'Yeah. Want to go to Superdrug?' she said, and I said okay.

For years I looked for her. In the street, on buses, in shops. I felt she would look exactly the same as she did when I was twelve. Even when I was almost definite it wasn't her, I had to check. Always a strange tugging of my heart when it wasn't her.

She moved to Nice with Brian, and wrote me letters that I didn't reply to. She remained, remains, colossal.

I graduated with a good maths degree. Dad and Peter, my boyfriend, came to the graduation. Dad stood in the middle of the aisle and took my picture. And then again, outside in the quadrangles, drinking complimentary Bucks Fizz, laughing, toasting the end of my university days. Even then, throughout the whole time, I could hear Mum say, in her tone of tender and complicated disappointment, 'Anyone can be a counter, Cara.'

O Tell Me The Truth
About Love!

I remember the night Shona met Brian. I was fourteen and Shona was nineteen, in her second year studying psychology. I had helped her get ready, as I always did. While she tried on outfits, I sat on the top bunk and issued helpful comments. She said I had to be honest. She'd rather I told her she looked chunky than have other people think it, secretly, when she was out. She was having a fat day and called herself a waddling hippo, a gross thing, and stared dismayed into the mirror.

'What are you talking about?' I said. 'You're gorgeous and clever and funny and nice. A boy would have to be off his noggin not to fancy you.'

Shona said I was only saying that 'cause I was her sister. She said she'd eaten two bags of crisps, a Double Decker, and a ham baguette on her way home from university.

'Everyone snacks too much at times,' I said, the voice of reason.

It distressed me when she talked this way. It made me sad that there was nothing I could say that would make her understand, finally and irrevocably, how wonderful she was. As far as I could see, Shona was as near perfect as anyone could be. She looked exactly like I wanted to look. Her hair was dyed pink, the colour of candyfloss, and she wore dramatic black round her eyes, and a lipstick called Vampire's Blood. That night, the night she met Brian, she wore baggy black combat trousers with a bicycle chain round them, and a red t-shirt with McShit written on it, a picture of a hamburger below. It was the fifth outfit she'd tried on. It took a lot of effort to look that casual. Then she put her hair up round her head in little twisted buns, and we smeared glitter up her arms and stuck stars on her cheeks with eyelash glue. The finishing touches were, for me, the most exciting part of the Shona-going-out process. They were imbued with magical transformative powers, and the potential for tragedy – the nights when she came home crying, mascara running down her face, and the glitter and stars still stuck on, sad remnants of the hope and excitement which had propelled her out the door a few hours earlier.

Before she left, I made us both a cup of tea and we sat in our room, talking. Shona did a psychological test on me, one she'd got from university, that rated personality in terms of sociability, ambition, materialism. She had great, almost religious, faith in them.

'It's scientific,' she said. '*Scientifically tested*. They use this in prison to discover if a person's a psychopath or not. Psychos don't blink,' she said. 'That's another indicator they use.'

'Really?' I said, and Shona nodded authoritatively. She told me some other interesting things she had learnt at university and said I was a fast learner since these were complicated ideas she was explaining to me. In the psychological test we both scored abnormally high neurotic levels. I was proud to be in the same league as Shona.

'Look,' she said, 'we're positively ricocheting off the list.'

'We *are* both worriers,' I said, and Shona said even if we didn't think we were, we were. 'This test is scientific, remember,' she said. 'It takes into account your unconscious.'

'Ah,' I said.

We finished our tea and Shona said she had to go. She said she'd much rather be staying home with me tonight, but she couldn't break her arrangements.

'Julie won't mind,' I said. 'Tell her you're ill.'

But Shona said she couldn't hide away at home for ever.

'Give me a guddle,' she said, and I did. 'Have a nice night, dolly dimples,' I said.

'You too, sweetie,' she said.

From the window I watched her go down the road, then I lay down for a while. *Blind Date* was on in the living room and I heard Mum laugh. I rolled my eyes, but there was no one there to see. When Shona was in we sometimes watched *Blind Date* with Mum. Shona said she was only interested in it from a sociological point of view – sociology was her other uni subject – and that Mum was a low-brow and Cilla Black an ignoramus. I wondered what I was going to do all night. Before Shona met Julie, she used to take me to the cinema on Saturday night and we saw eighteen-rated films and had a good laugh. I was a bit miffed at Julie for disrupting our Saturday night ritual, but I tried not to let it show. I hoped this going-out was a phase.

I got off the bed and tried on some clothes. Everything I owned was shabby and old-fashioned. Whatever I was, I felt sure my clothes didn't express it, and this was important if you wanted to attract the right boy for you. If the right boy did come along, he wouldn't recognize the inner me by my clothes, they'd give him the wrong impression. I tried on some of Shona's clothes – her MegaDeath t-shirt and a red bustier she wore on thin days – but they made me look foolish, like I was dressing up. On Shona they seemed to say something vital and important. They seemed to say something about her as a person, they made her stand out in the crowd in a singular and spectacular manner. Next I moved on to the mirror. Mum poked her head round the door and told me to stop gazabying at myself, and then left before I had time to reply.

'Go back to your telly,' I shouted, 'go back to sleep,' and I heard her laugh.

It was important to look at yourself objectively. You were meant to pick out your best feature and concentrate all your cosmetic energies on it. With Shona, it was her eyes. They sparkled under all the kohl she wore. My eyes were just there on my face, with no light in them, and my colouring was highly unstable, victim of the vicissitudes of heat and wind and social embarrassment. I looked like a farmer's daughter presiding over a cheese counter. The magazines said your smile was your greatest asset, but everyone knew that boys liked girls who didn't smile, who didn't speak much, and seemed unreachably aloof and mysterious. Someone who smiled all the time was no challenge.

At nine o'clock, feeling lonely, I watched *Who Wants To Be A Millionaire* with Mum. She had rubbed olive oil all over her face – she claimed it was cheaper and more effective than Oil of Olay – and had taken off her bra. This was what my Saturday nights had come to. I thought of the town – all the lights of the pubs blinking into the darkness and people laughing and drinking and having a great time – and wanted to cry. I asked Mum if she wanted a game of Monopoly and she said no.

'What d'you think Shona's doing right now?' I said, and Mum said enjoying herself, hopefully.

'She knows to be careful, anyway,' I said.

Dad came home from work and showed us a pair of slippers he'd bought in his lunch break. He was worried they looked like ladies' slippers, so he and Mum had a discussion about that. I went through to my room and wrote in my diary: *Saturday night. Mum and Dad discussing whether his new slippers look manly enough. Jesus wept. Shona out*, and then I couldn't think of anything else, and shut it. I settled in bed to wait for Shona. I started reading *Love for Lydia* again, my favourite book ever. I like the bit where he realizes Lydia's not just growing out of her clothes, but that she's wearing them a size too small deliberately, so people can see her figure. At some point I fell asleep, my cheek pressed against page ninety-six. I woke up at half three when Shona came into the room.

'Are you asleep?' she whispered, climbing onto the top bunk.

'Not any more,' I said and pulled back the sheets to let her in.

She told me that she'd met a boy at the Cathouse.

'We talked about everything,' she said. 'Just all night talking to each other.'

'Did you mention me?' I asked, and Shona said of course. She said she thought we would get on. He knows about Jung, and they talked about psychology and Freud.

'It was really interesting,' she said. 'He knows tons of stuff.'

'Who's Jung?' I said, but she waved me off and said it was too complicated to get into at this time of the night. She climbed down the ladder into her own bed, telling me he'd taken her number.

'I think he'll phone,' she said.

'Don't get your hopes up,' I said.

For a while she was quiet and I thought she was asleep. Then she said, 'He's got the *Carmina Burana* as his mobile phone ringsound.' She sounded delighted, and spoke with unselfconscious assurance that I found this delightful too.

'He sounds kind of silly,' I said. She needed sobering up.

Brian came over for tea three weeks later. He was wearing a black hat with a dent in it, and a t-shirt that said Love Sucks, with a vampire biting a woman's neck on it. I waited a bit in our room before coming out. Shona and Brian were on the couch, and Mum and Dad in an armchair each. Shona introduced him to me like she was unveiling a work of art, leaning back to give me a chance to register his awesomeness. I didn't think he was up to much. By the way she'd been talking about him, I was expecting a veritable sex god, not a lank-haired, podgy boy with white hands crossed delicately on his knees. The disparity between what he looked like in reality, and what I'd been led to believe, gave me some leverage, I felt, and I sauntered over to the couch and said, 'Hey.'

'Hey,' he said back.

There were a few minutes' silence, and Mum got up and said she'd put on the tea. I tried to look at Brian without being too obvious. Shona had told me the night before that she thought this was it, emphasising the 'it' so it came out in capital letters.

'It?' I said.

'You know. It. The real thing, the one.'

'How do you know?'

She said she just did. One day, she said, it would happen to me, and then I would know too. She said she'd met her fate, and I said that her fate might be to get run over tomorrow, you couldn't tell. She kept talking about his shoulders, how attractive they were, and how happy she felt being near him. Apart from anything else,

I was puzzled. I thought of the boys at school, when you saw them after gym and they had their t-shirts off. Their backs were white and pimpled, with bones jutting out, and the last thing I'd want to do is touch them. They looked clammy.

Dad asked him what he was doing at university, and Brian, not hurrying to answer, said third-year psychology and English.

'It's really the music I'm into,' he said, and Shona chipped in like a PR assistant to tell us he was in a band.

'What're you called?' I said, feeling neglected.

'You Will Know Us By the Trail of Blood,' said Brian. 'It's a tribute band.'

'Who're you tributing?'

'You Will Know Us By the Trail of *Dead*. We do our own stuff as well. You should come and see us rehearse some time,' he said, and I said I would. Dad said it didn't sound his cup of tea.

'Truth be told,' he said, 'we don't listen to much music. We like Neil Diamond,' he said. 'He's got a lot of good ones.'

Over tea, Mum asked Brian about getting his lip pierced, if it hurt, and Brian said no. She said she couldn't understand all these young people getting themselves perforated like that.

'Carla's the only sensible one out of you,' said Dad. 'She's only got her ears done.'

'Only 'cause you won't let me get anything else pierced,' I said, feeling aggrieved to be singled out for such ignominious praise. I tried to catch Shona's eye but she was either looking at her food or looking at Brian. He still hadn't taken off his hat and it perched like a vigilant canary on top of his head. Mum started up again, saying that young people will have ears like cauli-flowers soon, and then she got confused and said that wasn't the word she was looking for.

'What's the word I'm looking for?' she said, and a few long minutes passed. I heard Brian's fork scrape off his plate. He was eating single-mindedly, almost ferociously, as if nothing but his food could ever claim his attention.

'Colander!' Mum said at last. 'That's the word. Your bodies'll be like colanders soon.'

Shona said that since that was resolved, she and Brian would go upstairs, and I was left alone with Mum and Dad. They didn't say anything about Brian at all, and I was dumbfounded by their lack of interest.

'Was that panstick he was wearing?' I whispered, but Mum just shrugged and said, 'Was it? I didn't notice.'

I decided to go upstairs. After all, it was my room as well. As I reached the door, my defiant mood faltered a little, and I began to feel shy. I pushed the door slowly, to give them warning.

'What're you up to?' I said, quite casual, no big deal.

Brian was sitting on the chair beside our desk and Shona was crouched over him, putting black liner round his eyes. She said they were getting ready for Brian's gig tonight.

'Get many gigs, Brian?' I said, and he said just Hull town hall so far. 'It was a rocking crowd though,' he said.

He held the mirror close to him and said, 'Can you make it a bit curlier round the edges, babe?' and Shona said, 'No probs.'

I noticed the way her hand lay so casually on his thigh. I had to make a conscious effort to take my eyes away from it. I watched them get ready, and although Shona didn't ask my opinion, I told her her legs looked a bit plump in the skirt she was wearing. Brian said she looked great, and she beamed back at him and didn't seem to hear what I'd said. So much for honesty.

'Catch you later,' Brian said on their way out.

'Yeah,' I said.

Then they were gone. No pre-going-out chat with Shona, no guddle, no anything. I felt empty. Wrote in my diary: *Shona has discarded me like an old jumper. Brian is o.k. I'll still be here for her when all this has blown over.*

But it just got worse and worse. At least Julie only had Shona on Saturday night. Now Brian had her all weekend and during the week. When she was with me, it wasn't like the old days. She walked around with a secret smile on her face, and when I asked her what she was smiling about, she'd say, 'Oh, it's nothing. Just something Brian said last night.'

'What'd he say?'

'Oh, nothing. It wouldn't mean anything to *you*,' she'd say. 'Tell me what's been happening at school.'

'Okay. Wait here and I'll get us a cup of tea.'

I would bound down the stairs, preparing to unload myself and have a chat like we used to, and when I came back she'd be talking to him on the phone. They'd just talk rubbish, not Jung or anything, just telling each other what they'd had for tea or whatever. And now she called him sweetie and honey bun and dolly dimples, all the words we'd made up for each other, our private and special appellations. I felt deeply betrayed. Brian was ousting me.

It wasn't till after Christmas that I had a word with Mum. I happened to hint that I wondered if she really was staying over at Julie's.

'It's her uni work I'm worried about,' I said regretfully, almost sadly. 'I think it's suffering.'

My Machiavellian plan went horribly wrong and culminated in Shona moving into Brian's for good. She packed up her stuff in a jubilant mood, saying I'd done her a good turn, it was what they both wanted anyway.

'You're leaving and you're looking so happy about it,' I said, trailing her round the room. I was nearly crying with the immensity of the unfolding drama. When she un-tacked her David Bowie poster I knew my fate was sealed, and my life was destroyed. She sat me down and told me she was only going to the West End, only a bus ride away.

'Come up any time,' she said. 'Whenever you want to chat, or get away from Tweedledum and Tweedledee, just come up.'

'It's not the same,' I said.

She said this was part of growing up, and she had to make a life of her own. 'You'll understand when it happens to you,' she said, and I said I was sick of that mantra.

'It's true, though,' she said.

In my diary I wrote: *Shona is gone for good. Too depressed to write.*

It turned out I saw Shona just as much as before. She came back to do their washing and they both came over for Sunday lunch. She bought me a mobile phone for my birthday so we could text each other.

It was a few weeks before I went round to their flat. Brian's parents had bought it for him, right in the middle of Great Western Road. The rooms were draughty and smelt of stale incense. Shona took me out to the Asian fruit shops and exclaimed over the fresh coriander. She made a curry when we went home, bustling about the kitchen in a businesslike manner. I was shocked. At home she'd never made anything that involved chopping or stirring. She'd been adamant that women shouldn't cook. (Cooking was the thin end of the wedge. If you cooked, you had to start washing pots and pans, wiping surfaces, and before you knew it you'd be knee-deep in domestic duties.) To top it all off, she started telling me about a new super Vileda mop they'd bought. It meant she didn't have to scrub the kitchen floor on her hands and knees any more.

'You scrub the kitchen floor on your hands and knees?' I said, and she said yeah. She didn't want rats or anything getting attracted to the crumbs.

'On your hands and knees?' I said, and Shona said it wasn't a cardinal sin. 'Brian has weak knees,' she said.

'You've really changed, Shona,' I said, sounding more accusatory than I meant. 'You've forgotten your principles and ideals.'

Shona laughed. She said that when you loved someone you wanted to take care of them, and Brian took care of her, as she did him.

'He cooks and cleans as well,' she said.

She spoke to me now as if I was much younger than her and still had a lot to learn. I said she sounded like one of those lobotomized American self-help gurus. I told her I was going to get a man who did everything for me, I'd be totally free of domestic constraints, and Shona said, 'You thunk so?'

'I thunk so,' I said, although privately I wasn't so confident that anyone would ever love me, or that I would love anyone. Shona said it didn't sound very fair, and I told her it'd be historical compensation.

'We'll see,' she said.

Brian came home, angry about a bad mark he'd got for his Freud essay. He said that when he'd started the course, he'd intended to break the psychology world from the inside. He'd get accepted into their fold and then one day he'd stand up and say, *There, you bastards, you thought I was one of you, but I'm not.*

'Why don't you like the psychology world?' I said, and Brian said it was too conservative. I asked him in what way, but he pretended not to hear me, and I realized he didn't know. I looked over at Shona, who winked at me, and that made me feel good. For a few minutes we were a team again.

It wasn't that I didn't like Brian. He was quite nice and treated me like we were both on the same side. He was very serious, but I didn't think he was very bright, so his seriousness struck me as faintly comical. He spoke slowly, with a lot of pregnant pauses, and I found it frustrating waiting for him to get to his point. Sometimes I wanted to shake him and say, 'Come on, Bri, spit it out!'

After *Coronation Street* we went to a pub called the Halt Bar to meet up with some of their friends. Shona said I'd better sit at the back of the table, so none of the staff saw me.

'What are you imbibing?' said Brian, and I was stumped. I'd never been in a pub before.

'I'm having vodka soda lime,' said Shona. 'It's low-calorie.'

'I'll have one of those, then,' I said.

There were about ten people at the table. I was sitting beside Big George. He was dressed in black – they all were – with PVC trousers that screeched every time he moved. He had his hair in a ponytail, and a big face that appeared monstrously larger than life, swollen, and covered in white make-up that made his plainness touching. The first thing he said to me was that his trousers were chafing him.

'It's my weight,' he said. 'How much overweight d'you think I am?'

He stared straight at me, and I blushed and said he didn't look too heavy. He insisted I put a figure on it, so I said, 'A few pounds?'

'Two stones seven pounds,' he said, sounding satisfied with the precision of the figure. He told me he was a computer programmer, twenty-nine, and lived with his mum. He rubbed his hands together, in what I supposed to be a parody of a lecherous old man, and said I looked young.

'I'm sixteen,' I said, a number which sounded more acceptable than fourteen. I took a cigarette from him, saying, 'What the hell.' It felt strange and glamorous, holding it with my elbow rested on the table, and the few vodkas making me feel dreamy. I was half aware that I could practise my powers of seduction on Big George, him being so old and therefore out of the picture as far as any romantic possibility was concerned. I tucked my head down and looked at him from under my eyelashes, but Shona nudged me from across the table and asked me if I was okay.

Big George asked me a lot of questions, and then answered them himself. He made me feel the sweat on his inner thigh – *It's sweltering in here*, he said. *Feel this*, and he grabbed my hand and put it on his PVC-ed thigh – and I said yes, it was hot.

'Have you seen any good films?' he said.

I looked over at Shona, trying to plead with her, soundlessly, to save me, but she was kissing Brian. I'd never seen them kiss before. I looked over at an empty leather booth by the window, with a candle and a lonely flickering flame, and wished I was sitting there with someone I wanted to kiss.

'*Cinema Paradiso*'s good,' I said. I like films with subtitles. (In fact it was the only film with subtitles I'd ever seen, but I felt sure I would enjoy other subtitled films.)

Big George started telling me about his favourite film. It was to do with a woman getting murdered by having her head banged off a photocopier.

'And the cool thing is,' said Big George, 'that you can see every stage of the murder. 'Cause the photocopier's on, and it's taking pictures of it.'

'I don't like the sound of that,' I said, and Big George leaned over and whispered, 'Are you wearing stockings?' into my ear.

'No,' I said, leaning back. He came even closer and said, 'I bet you're a virgin.'

I stayed the night at Shona and Brian's. After they'd gone to bed I got out my diary and wrote: *So much has happened*, but then I couldn't be bothered to write anything down. *I wore my azure cardigan and my rosebud skirt, and my new brown shoes with the strap across the ankle. I'll describe what happened tomorrow. It was an experience anyway, and that's what counts.* As an afterthought I added, *Shona has turned into a housewife.* And then, *Love is an institution that oppresses women.*

I couldn't sleep for a long time. In the dark I listened to the silence of the flat, wondering if Brian and Shona were having sex. In films couples always made a lot of noise when they were having sex, but I didn't know if that was a necessary condition of the act, or a contrivance of film-makers. The flat was absolutely still and quiet, and I fell asleep not knowing either way.

About six months into their living together, I got a phone call from Shona at ten o'clock at night. At first I couldn't hear her because she was weeping and wailing, and trying to talk in between. She was meant to be meeting Brian and his friends (although they were her friends too, now) in the pub, and she was all dressed up, waiting for him to call and tell her where they were, and he hadn't phoned.

'And I've binged,' she said. 'I just ate five Tunnocks wafers and a pizza.'

'Oh, Shona,' I said.

I remember when Shona was thirteen, on the night of her

school disco, and her friend Hazel had gone with other people, but not told Shona. Shona was waiting in the house for her to arrive, and it was only at eight o'clock that she accepted Hazel wasn't going to turn up. I remember her standing in the living room with her hair curled and her red ra-ra skirt, with her hands by her sides, and she was crying. But every few seconds she would stop and try to smile, but it looked painful, like a muscle contraction. And I'd hated Hazel then like I hated Brian now.

'Right,' I said, in control. 'Get a taxi down to Mum's.'

Shona said she couldn't do that. She said he might be hurt, or something might have happened and, even if nothing had happened, she wanted to hear his explanation anyway. Thwarted, but not defeated, I told her to calm down, to talk me through it, but I couldn't hear her through her sobs.

'I wish I could give you a guddle,' I said, and she laughed and started crying afresh.

'*I* love you,' I said, 'would *I* treat you like that?' and she had to say no.

In the middle of telling me how selfish he was, Brian came in and Shona said she had to go. She put the phone down. I lay in bed, tense, feeling curiously excited. Black clouds puttered over the sky. I didn't know what was the right thing to say in this sort of situation, and considered asking Mum, but decided against it. I felt this was my experience, and I didn't want other people appropriating a piece of it as their own. It had been an excessive reaction for Shona to have, I admitted, but then who knew what had been going on these past few months. Maybe she'd been suffering in silence all along, scared to let me see because I'd told her this would happen. I wouldn't reproach her.

At midnight she phoned again, still crying. They'd had a terrible fight. Brian had come home with a flimflam excuse about forgetting the time, and Shona had gone mad. She really gave it to him, but then he had the cheek to start having a go at her.

'He started screaming "Fuck your cuppas",' said Shona. '*Fuck your cuppas*, just 'cause I mentioned that I always take him a cup of tea in the morning, and it'd be nice for him to do that for me one day.'

I said that was outrageous. I said he didn't know how lucky he was to have Shona, and she snivelled and said, 'I know.'

'You don't see his dark side,' she said, and I said no, but I could imagine.

'He's a big useless lump, anyway,' I said.

I told her I'd come over tomorrow and we could bring some of her stuff back to Mum's. Shona said it wasn't that easy.

'You'll get over it,' I said. 'Remember that swimming triathlon? You said you were going to die when you came in last for that, number 99 remember? Behind all those old biddies? You said you'd never get over that, remember. But you did, didn't you? It's just like that.'

Shona said it wasn't like that at all, and I said I knew that, but it was the same principle. She sighed as if she were sick of listening to me.

'I need to talk to him,' she said.

'Sometimes the talking has to stop,' I said.

I got out my diary, feeling I should document what had happened. *Stop Press*, I wrote. *How can someone who's supposed to love you say you eat like a pig (even though he looks like a pig himself)???*

I was full of vim the next morning. It was a Saturday, so I got up early and prepared to go over to Shona's. I told Mum not to count her chickens, but that Shona might be back with us very soon.

'She's coming home?' Mum said. 'She's not said anything to me.'

'They've had a fight,' I said, enigmatically. 'A big one,' I said, and raised my eyebrows.

Mum said I should give them some space to work things out themselves, but I told her Shona needed me. She was ready to move on. Mum said maybe she should come with me, and I said no.

'Leave it to me,' I said.

At the bus stop I phoned to see if Shona wanted me to bring anything up. She sounded surprised to hear from me.

'We're just about to have a bath,' she said.

'Together?' I said.

'Yip. Oh, sorry about last night,' she said. 'I got a bit carried away.'

I said I couldn't believe it. He treated her like a skivvy, made her so upset, and now she was jumping into a bath with him.

'I've heard it all now,' I said, and she said she was sorry, she was just letting off steam last night. I asked her if they always took baths together and she giggled and said sometimes.

'It can't be good if you need a clean,' I said, and Shona thought I was joking and laughed. I thought about how self-conscious she was about her body, and how she'd never let me see her naked.

She said would I mind not coming over. She and Brian were going to spend the day together, and I said not to let me stop them. She didn't seem to notice I was angry.

'Thanks, duckie,' she said.

I went home and watched *Countdown* with Mum. I told her I'd had it with Shona and her love life, and Mum said I'd just have to wait and get one of my own.

'No way,' I said. 'She's put me off relationships for good.'

'Is that right,' said Mum.

'I'm going to be a lesbian,' I said, and Mum said good, variety was the spice of life.